TWISTED TRAIL

Cleef Morgan was a Pinkerton detective at the top of his grim career so it came as no surprise when he was sent after Scrag Hanton, the killer and bank robber. Hanton died resisting arrest and so Morgan had succeeded yet again. Then the call from Turkey Creek came and Morgan was faced with a mystery that had baffled the local lawmen. It was just another job to Morgan, and he set about unravelling the track of deceit. His life lay in the balance, but he would never quit until he had brought justice with gun or hang-rope.

Books by Corba Sunman
in the Linford Western Library:

RANGE WOLVES
LONE HAND
GUN TALK
TRIGGER LAW
GUNSMOKE JUSTICE
BIG TROUBLE
GUN PERIL
SHOWDOWN AT
SINGING SPRINGS

CORBA SUNMAN

TWISTED TRAIL

Complete and Unabridged

LINFORD
Leicester

First published in Great Britain in 2004 by
Robert Hale Limited
London

First Linford Edition
published 2005
by arrangement with
Robert Hale Limited
London

British Library CIP Data

Sunman, Corba
    Twisted Trail.—Large print ed.—
Linford western library
1. Western stories
2. Large type books
I. Title
823.9'14 [F]

ISBN 1–84395–807–4

Published by
F. A. Thorpe (Publishing)
Anstey, Leicestershire

Set by Words & Graphics Ltd.
Anstey, Leicestershire
Printed and bound in Great Britain by
T. J. International Ltd., Padstow, Cornwall

This book is printed on acid-free paper

1

Cleef Morgan was taking pains to travel unseen across the barren land in south-west Texas. He lived by the tenet that the man who anticipated trouble could never be taken completely by surprise. He had an instinct for cover and took advantage of any that nature provided, staying clear of high ground and skylines and avoiding all likely ambush spots. Many clumps of mesquite thick enough to conceal an attacker dotted the landscape, and he looked ahead longingly at the low, brushy hills that promised a break in the monotonous flatness that had existed for many miles.

Yet he was following faint sign through this seemingly deserted country — a hoofprint here, a broken twig of mesquite there — remorselessly trailing Scrag Hanton, bank robber and killer, who had finally made a mistake in the planning of his seventh bank robbery in a notorious career that had spanned years of wanton killing and vicious disrespect of life and limb. Such was the degree of Hanton's evil skill in evading capture that the local law had sent an appeal to the Pinkerton National Detective Agency for a man capable of the necessary violence to apprehend the desperate outlaw.

Cleef Morgan, whose peerless reputation as a manhunter struck fear into the black hearts of those he pursued relentlessly to an inevitable climax, had been the obvious choice for the grim chore, and a month had elapsed since he took up the case. In that time he had studied Hanton's methods and learned much about the outlaw's way of life. He had delved into Hanton's past and questioned those who had been unfortunate enough to become victims in the outlaw's crooked forays, building up a picture of the fugitive while following the wispy signs that marked the progress of his violent career. The recent bank raid at Greenville, in which two men and a woman had been shot down in cold blood by the escaping robber, had given Morgan a fresh trail to follow, and now he was closing in on the thieving killer who had proved too difficult for the local law to handle.

Tall in the saddle, Morgan wore a sun-faded grey Stetson pulled low over blue eyes. His angular face was well tanned, rugged, with a prominent chin set with thrusting determination. A profusion of small scars, showing white through the sweat on his weathered visage, had accumulated around his eyes and on his cheeks, stark testament to the many tough cases he had solved. His long nose was straight, unbroken despite the battles he had fought for the law. There was confidence and defiance in every angle of his tough, powerful body, his confidence arising out of his successful past.

Faded blue denim pants encased his long legs. He was wearing brown Justin boots. A leather vest covered the dark cotton shirt stretched across his massive chest. He was four inches over six feet in height, an intimidating figure in a harsh world where tough men abounded. At thirty-two, he looked several years older, a lean, taciturn man who lived for his job and did it without fear or favour. He carried a Winchester carbine in a scabbard on the right side of his horse, the butt protruding conveniently near to hand, and had a Smith & Wesson .44 pistol in a greased holster tied down on his right thigh. Despite his travel-stained appearance, both his weapons were spotlessly clean and ready for instant use.

He rode steadily throughout the long day, halting several times to rest his horse. His alertness was constant. He watched the faint trail he was following, drawn along as if attached to it by a rope. As evening drew on he became even more cautious, aware that Hanton would settle down somewhere ahead and watch his backtrail for signs of pursuit. Morgan had noted the general direction the robber was taking and assumed the man was making for the Mexican border. He judged that Hanton was barely an hour ahead of him.

Just before full dark, when he could no longer pick out the faint trail he was following, Morgan halted and made camp, apparently ignoring his surroundings as he took care of his horse and then himself. He lit a small fire to boil water for coffee, ate cold food, then rolled himself in his blanket and waited for full darkness to settle.

When the night became so black it was impossible to see a hand raised before his eyes, Morgan slid out of the blanket and removed his boots. In the darkness he worked by touch alone, covering his saddle and some brush-wood with the blanket, then arranging his boots to protrude as if they were still on his feet. Finally he stuck his hat on the saddle as if it were covering his face. Satisfied, he moved off to a rock only a couple of yards away which he had noted before making camp. He drew his .44 and held it uncocked in his right hand, then fell to watching the campsite, certain that Hanton would come calling. He remained motionless in the interminable night, tired but alert, silent and deadly as a rattler . . .

The sky to the east had lost its blackest density and taken on the lighter hue of nearing dawn when Morgan heard a faint sound close at hand. At first he thought it was made by a small animal, but then he noted a slight changing of darkness patterns and strained his eyes until he picked up the indistinct shape of a man crawling into the camp. He did not move but lifted his pistol to cover the figure, leaving the weapon uncocked, his finger steady on the trigger.

The man took a long time to cover the short distance to the humped blanket, which, to Morgan's critical gaze, looked as if it contained a sleeping man. He could just make out the toes of his boots protruding from under the bottom of the blanket, and liked the little touch that gave reality to his trap. Finally, the crawling man reared up and hurled himself upon the blanket-covered saddle, his right arm rising and falling swiftly, his long-bladed hunting knife striking viciously.

Morgan cocked his pistol at that instant, the faint sound bringing the man swinging around fast, although he must have been shocked when the point of his blade struck obdurate leather instead of finding a man's heart. But his instincts were those of a wild animal as he turned at bay.

'Hold it, Hanton,' Morgan rasped. 'I'm a Pinkerton. I got you covered. Get your hands up where I can see them or you're dead. I got you to rights.'

Hanton froze. On his hands and knees, he was at a disadvantage with the knife in his right hand and his pistol in its holster. He dropped the knife, the pale blur of his face turned towards Morgan, his teeth showing in a baleful snarl, like a brown bear interrupted at his first meal after long hibernation.

'I heard you was on my tail, Morgan,' Hanton rasped. 'And they said you was tricky. So you got me cold, but it's a long ways to the nearest law office. Something tells me one of us ain't gonna reach it, and I sure as hell reckon it's you.'

'Get up and keep your hands away from your belt,' Morgan said tersely. 'It don't matter to me one way or the other how you get to that law office, sitting your saddle or lying face-down across it. That's up to you. If you figure this is your lucky day then make a play for your gun. Make me kill you and I'll do it with great pleasure.'

Hanton got to his feet, staggering a little, and then swung to face Morgan, his right hand moving with the speed of a striking rattler. He grasped the butt of his pistol and it came out of leather fast. Morgan shook his head sadly as he heard the weapon click into the cocked position. He squeezed off a shot that smashed into Hanton's chest, boring through the outlaw's heart as the impact knocked him off balance and flung him carelessly to the ground. Morgan straightened his cramped limbs and arose stiffly. He stalked forward to inspect his kill, his deadly gun covering the inert figure, the smell of gunsmoke reeking in his nostrils while the crash of his shot yet lingered in his ears.

They never learned, he told himself. Desperation almost always brought resistance from the badmen he pursued, although they didn't have the remotest chance of beating a cold drop. He bent over the outlaw, removing weapons instinctively, although he knew where his slug had struck the man. Straightening, he stifled a yawn. It had been a long, soul-destroying night and he felt gaunted inside. He blinked as the sun took a one-eyed peek over the horizon and filled his tired eyes with golden fire.

Holstering his gun, Morgan pulled on his boots and crossed to his brown stallion to unhook his canteen from the saddle horn. He took a long swig of brackish water, his keen eyes on the inert body of the outlaw. Daylight was coming fast now, lengthening his range of vision. The sun was clearing the horizon, highlighting the grim scene of a man sprawled dead, his vicious trail having reached its inevitable end, his executioner standing tall and resolute, preparing to go on about his dangerous business.

Morgan had no regrets as he ate cold food from his dwindling supplies, feeling only a sense of deep satisfaction every time his gaze alighted upon the inert body of the outlaw. Hanton took his score of dead badmen to twelve, and he had arrested more than twenty men during his impressive career, most of whom had died on the gallows in grim payment for their crimes. Relief was the only emotion he felt when a case ended. But he could never forget the ghastly moment when, as a impressionable boy of ten years, he had run to the bank in

Newton, Kansas, in response to the sound of gunfire, to find his father, a bank teller, lying dead in a widening pool of his own blood.

That moment had discoloured his life, gave him a grim purpose which he had followed rigidly during the ensuing years. He made inexorable war on bad men, intent upon ridding the world of their evil presence, and working for the law had proved to be the perfect way of satisfying his compulsion. At eighteen he had become a deputy marshal in Dodge City, learning much of what he knew from Wyatt Earp himself, then moving on, goaded by the never to be forgotten sight of his father lying dead, cut off in the prime of life by a robber's cruel bullet.

He broke camp and rode along the last tracks Hanton had made until he found the outlaw's horse picketed in the brush a mile away. He returned to Hanton and threw the body across the saddle, covering it with a blanket and roping it in place. It was only then that he gave thought to his whereabouts, and judged that Juniper Bend was some ten miles to the north-west. He felt slightly light-headed from hunger and lack of sleep as he touched spurs to his mount and went on, hardly able to remember the last time he had eaten a cooked meal. But for days now his stomach had been warning that it had been too long, and for once he felt a yearning for the comforts of a town and the relaxation it could bring.

Juniper Bend was a fair-sized town of some 300 inhabitants, serving the needs of the local ranches and the many travellers who passed through on their way along the southern route into California. Morgan reined in at the head of the main street and gazed impassively along its wide length. The place looked half-asleep in the bright sunlight, with only a scattering of saddle horses tethered here and there and a couple of wagons outside a store.

Morgan rode into the town until he reached the law office. He stepped down stiffly from his saddle, stretched his powerful body and flexed his knees, then looked swiftly around to locate an eating-house. A grunt of satisfaction escaped him when he spotted a sign fifty yards along the street, advertising culinary expertise. He strode into the law office and confronted an oldish man who was seated with elbows on a desk, his cupped hands holding up his head while he snored loudly. There was a sheriff's badge pinned to the man's shirt front.

Morgan went to the desk and slapped the top with a heavy hand. The sheriff snorted and roused himself, looking up with bleary eyes, frowning as he considered the massive figure confronting him.

'Whadda you want?' he demanded grumpily. 'What's so damn important you got to come barging in here at this time o' the day?'

'You ever heard of an outlaw name of Scrag Hanton?' Morgan asked.

The sheriff leaned back in his chair.

'Sure have, and I'd give a month's pay to set eyes on him.'

'You can see him for nothing.' Morgan permitted himself a brief grin. 'He's outside, face down across his bronc.'

'Dead?'

Morgan nodded. 'And ready for burying.'

The sheriff gazed at him in disbelief, then got up and ran to the door to peer outside. When he saw the blanket-covered figure on the horse he threw a quick glance at Morgan, before going out for a closer look. He lifted a corner of the blanket and peered intently at Hanton, then, shaking his head in disbelief, came back into the office.

'You kill him?' he demanded.

'At daybreak, about ten miles from here.'

'You some kind of a lawman? I don't see no badge on you.'

'Pinkerton man. Name of Cleef Morgan. The sheriff of Pelo County hired me to get Hanton.'

'Say, I've heard of you.' The sheriff's manner thawed perceptibly. 'You was over in this neck of the woods about three years ago. Nailed Bart Forbes and his two sidekicks after they knocked over the Denton stage. Wells Fargo brought you in that time. Neat piece of work! And now you've done for Scrag Hanton. I'm Hank Teal, Morgan, and I'm right pleased to make your acquaintance. If there's anything I can do for you while you're here then just say the word.'

'Take care of Hanton's body while I get myself a beer and a meal,' Morgan said. 'I been on the trail for several weeks.'

'Sure thing. Leave it to me. You'll send a wire to Pelo County, huh, telling them about this?'

'All in good time.' Morgan turned to the door. 'Right now I need some time to myself, and the minute I declare my whereabouts the office will send me instructions for another case. I'll ride into Pelo County before announcing

15

Hanton's death. It's the only way I can get some peace. I'm in great demand these days.'

He left the office and Teal accompanied him to the sidewalk.

'You're toting Hanton all the way to Pelo County?' the sheriff demanded.

'Mebbe not. I'll wire my office after I've cleaned up and had a bite to eat. I'll feel different then. Right now I'm like a prairie dog that's been trapped in its hole for a month.'

He turned away and caught up the reins of his brown stallion, swinging into the saddle with a lithe movement that gave no hint of his intense tiredness. He hoped he would get the chance to rest. He had begun to figure that he was the only detective working for Pinkerton, the way they kept throwing new cases at him. He rode along the street to the livery barn and handed his horse over to an ostler, giving strict instructions for the animal's care. He removed his spurs and tucked them into a saddle-bag before throwing the twin bags across his shoulder.

He walked along the street, paused at the door of the eating-house and cast a glance longingly at an adjacent saloon. But his thirst could wait, he decided, and entered the food parlour. He spent thirty minutes regaling himself with good food and finished the meal with two cups of coffee. Then, grunting with satisfaction, he arose to visit the saloon, where he took a glass of beer to a table and sat composing a report for his office. As he was draining his glass of cold beer the batwings were thrust open and Sheriff Teal came hurrying in.

'Thought I'd find you in here,' Teal remarked. 'I've put Hanton in the undertaker's parlour until you decide what to do with him.' He sat down opposite Morgan and looked with interest at the report.

'You can read it.' Morgan pushed the report across the table and watched the sheriff's expressive face as the man perused it. There was something akin to hero-worship in the local lawman's face when he looked up.

'It musta taken a lot of cold nerve, waiting through the night for Hanton to show like that. You sure are one helluva manhunter.' Teal spoke with enthusiasm. 'Hanton ran us all ragged in this area. He made our lives a misery, having to chase out after him when we got word of his whereabouts, which hardly ever proved to be right. We never got a sight of him, but he sure made his mark on several towns around here. He was not satisfied with stealing. He had to kill innocent folk while he was doing it, and it didn't matter to him if he gunned down men or women.'

'Well he's gone now.' Morgan felt a sense of deep satisfaction. He arose from the table and picked up the report. 'I better send this so they know where I am, and I'll have to stick around town until I get a reply.' He picked up his saddle-bags.

'I'll walk with you to the telegraph office.' Teal arose and followed Morgan to the batwings.

Morgan was tired. The past month on the trail had expended his nervous energy and he needed a respite from the high pinnacle of alertness and performance which attended his job. He went to the telegraph office and sent his wire to the Chicago office, with a duplicate to the sheriff of Pelo County, who had requested his services in the first place. He sighed with relief as he walked back along the street to the hotel, where he booked a room and a bath, and was glad to escape to the privacy of the room, leaving Sheriff Teal in the lobby.

Before he could relax he cleaned his pistol, and took a long time over the weapon, for his life depended upon its efficiency. He had a change of clothes in his saddle-bags and shook the creases from the garments. Then he went for a bath, and shaved the thick black stubble off his angular face before returning to his room. He jammed the back of a chair under the door handle, sank down on the bed and surrendered to sleep.

Much later a hammering on the door jerked him awake. He lay for some moments gathering his thoughts while the fist continued to pound the thin panel. He cursed roundly, and a sigh escaped him when he pushed his big frame off the bed. He lit the lamp, and snaked his pistol out of its holster.

'Who in hell is it?' he called.

'Sheriff Teal. You got a reply from Chicago. I brought it along in case it was urgent.'

Morgan grimaced and opened the door. 'You could have let me sleep till morning,' he complained. 'What time is it?'

'Close to midnight. You've had more than enough sleep.' Teal produced a yellow envelope and thrust it at Morgan. 'This could be important.'

Morgan took the envelope. 'It's always important. And so is my sleep. I'll read it in the morning. Goodnight.'

He closed the door and replaced the chair back under the handle. Returning to the bed, he flopped down on it and closed his eyes, gripping the envelope in his hand. But the desire to sleep had receded, and he sighed and sat up, now fully awake. Gazing at the envelope, he tore it open and read the wire.

MORGAN, JUNIPER BEND, TEXAS. REF. HANTON. CONGRATULATIONS ON JOB WELL DONE. PHOTOGRAPH HANTON FOR IDENTIFICA- TION PURPOSES BEFORE BURIAL. NEW ASSIGNMENT URGENT. LOCATION, TURKEY CREEK, LATIMER COUNTY, TEXAS. REPORT TO SHERIFF CASSIDY SOONEST AND CONFIRM ARRIVAL TO THIS OFFICE. GOOD LUCK. SOURCE AND ORIGIN: T.J. MARSTON, HEAD OFFICE, CHICAGO.

Morgan read the wire twice then threw it aside. Where in hell was Turkey

Creek? And he had never heard of Latimer County. He opened a saddle-bag and took out a large-scale map of Texas, poking it with a long forefinger as he searched for the new location. A sigh escaped him when he found Latimer County, some 200 miles north of his present position. He flopped back on his pillow and resolutely closed his eyes.

The next morning he attended to the closing details of the Hanton case, took his leave of Sheriff Teal, and rode north. In the middle of the afternoon on the fifth day he topped a ridge and reined in to look down upon the sprawling township of Turkey Creek, a community of some 400 souls whose existence depended mainly on ranching.

He pushed on and entered the wide main street, jogging along until he spotted the law office sited between a bank and a store. His first impression was that Turkey Creek looked dead. The street was deserted. There was just a single horse tied to a hitching rail in front of a saloon a block away. He dismounted, wondering what kind of trouble was plaguing the local sheriff. The law office looked like it had been closed for months, and he frowned when he spotted several bullet holes in the door. The windows were dusty.

Morgan reached out to open the door, and at that instant the thud of hoofs sounded along the street. He looked round and saw six riders emerging from the livery barn. They came at a gallop along the street, and the next instant the town reverberated to the raucous sound of gunfire as they drew their guns and began shooting wildly in the air. Morgan thrust open the door of the office and practically fell inside. He slammed the door and ducked, for several bullets thudded into the woodwork, one passing through and spanging off the iron stove across the room, narrowly missing Morgan's head in passing.

He hit the floor hard, and looked around as the riders hammered on out of town, their shouts and screeching fading abruptly. He saw a man seated at a desk in a corner, oldish, with a law star pinned to his vest, regarding him stolidly, unperturbed by the shots. Morgan got to his feet slowly, hitching his gunbelt as he approached the desk. So his first impression was wrong, he thought as he dusted himself down. There was big trouble in this community, and he was embroiled in it before he had any idea what was wrong.

2

The sheriff looked as if he had taken root in his seat. He regarded Morgan with unblinking brown eyes, his demeanour suggesting that the shooting incident was normal in this town. He was not young, around the fifty mark, with a long nose and a thin mouth. If the troubled expression on his gaunt face was anything to go by, thought Morgan, then he was a very worried man.

'What was that disturbance all about?' Morgan demanded, his ears still ringing from the shooting. He was mindful of the fact that the sheriff had not stirred at all.

'That was the HW outfit on its way back to home range. They buried one of their crew on Boot Hill this afternoon. He was shot in the back the night before last. Who are you, mister, and what's your business in town?'

'The name is Cleef Morgan. It should mean something to you.'

'Cleef Morgan.' The sheriff scratched his stubbled chin. 'Yeah. Strikes a note in my mind. Where do I know you from? I don't reckon your face. We ain't met before, have we?'

'Never.' Morgan shook his head. 'I'm a Pink sent in response to your request for help. So what's your problem?'

'A Pink? Now what in hell is that?'

'Pinkerton man. You wired the agency in Chicago. I got here soon as I could.'

'Waal, you sure took your time, huh? I sent that wire more than a month ago. Gave up any hope of seeing some of those slick Pinkerton operators.'

'Like I said, I got here soon as I could.' Morgan shrugged his heavy shoulders. 'I had to finish the case I was handling before coming on to Turkey Creek. What's your name? I was told to report to Tom Cassidy.'

'That's me, right enough. Been

sheriff of Latimer County for more years than I care to remember. How many men have you brung along?'

'How many? Sheriff, I'm the whole caboodle.' Morgan permitted himself a grin. 'You only got one heap of trouble, huh? So that's why you got just one operative.' He pulled a chair to the desk and sat down. 'Give me the lowdown on your problem.'

Cassidy shook his head slowly. 'This ain't gonna work,' he mused. 'I reckon an army couldn't handle this situation, and they've sent me one man.'

'Feed me the details and let me be the judge. I can send for another man if I feel the case needs extra help.'

'Another man? Jeez, I need real help here, f'chris'sakes!'

'Yeah, I'd say you do.' Morgan spoke coolly. 'You didn't stir a muscle when that shooting broke out. So just tell me what your problem is and I'll sort it while you go back to sleep.'

Cassidy gazed at him for some moments, his eyes showing that he was under strain. Then he nodded slowly. 'On the face of it there ain't much to tell. Gus Mulder owns the Big G ranch; the biggest in the county. He came into town about five weeks ago and robbed the bank, killing Lew Wishart, the banker, in the process. Mulder and more than twenty thousand dollars went missing, and neither have been seen since. That's it in a nutshell. I ran myself ragged looking for Mulder, but he's disappeared into thin air. Nobody's seen hide or hair of him since the night of the robbery.'

'The night of the robbery?' Morgan frowned. 'In my experience, banks are usually robbed during business hours.'

'Yeah, and that's where it gets a mite involved. First off, Mulder owns the biggest ranch in the county, which means he ain't short of a dollar. Why in hell he robbed the bank is a mystery to me. I've known him for many years, and he's never put a foot wrong. Didn't have to. But he came into town that night to play poker with his cronies, one of them being Wishart, the banker, and talked Wishart into taking him into the bank for a withdrawal. According to the other card-players, the pair were gone some time, and then there was a couple of shots. An investigation revealed Wishart lying dead in the bank and the safe cleaned out. Mulder was gone as well as the dough and, like I said, he ain't been seen since.'

Morgan nodded slowly. 'Looks like an open and shut case,' he mused, 'and that type is usually the hardest to solve.' He reached into a breast pocket and produced a notebook and a pencil. 'Who was playing poker that night, and where were they playing?'

'They allus played in Wishart's apartment over the bank. It was a regular thing for them to meet there on Saturday evenings — have done for years. It was an exclusive game. Just Wishart, Mulder, Jonas Draper the lawyer who also owns the hotel, Sam Ashby, who owns the store, the saloon, and the livery stable, and Hank

Whiteman, whose HW outfit were firing their pistols as they left town just now. That bunch was showing its disrespect for the law because Mulder ain't been caught or the bank money recovered.'

Morgan wrote down the information, nodding slowly as he did so. He looked up at the sheriff's intent face. 'You said the HW outfit was in town today, burying one of their outfit. Who died? Where was he shot? Did you get the killer?'

'Whip Taylor got plugged. He was riding night guard on HW range when it happened. There's been trouble of one kind or another most nights out there. Night riders are working under cover of darkness, scaring folks, shooting up some spreads, and even gunning down cattle. That's all I can tell you. I've been out on the range night and day and never learned a thing about the setup.'

'When did the night riding start? Before or after the bank was robbed?'

Cassidy shook his head, eyes narrowed as he considered. 'About the same time, I guess. Can't rightly say. There was too much going on at that time. I got just two deputies, Mike Bradley and Frank Truscott. Mike's around town someplace. Have a word with him. He might be able to tell you more. But like I say, there's too much for this department to handle. I did a routine investigation and came up with nothing beyond the fact that Wishart was killed and the cash stolen. The town council voted that we bring in Pinkerton to sort this out.'

'I'll get around to questioning the witnesses, but tell me what you think happened. I reckon you have a personal opinion, huh? You know the kind of thing I mean. You get all the available evidence, which seems to point in a particular direction, but you get a feeling that it happened some other way.'

Cassidy shook his head. 'No,' he said. 'I don't know what the hell could have happened if the witnesses told it different from how it was. And why would they lie about it? Five of the top men in the town were playing cards like they'd done every week for months, and that particular evening one of them kicks over the traces, robs the bank and kills the banker. I came up against a brick wall, Morgan, and I ain't clever enough to see through it.'

Morgan nodded, studying the notes he had made. His eyes were bright when he looked at Cassidy. 'Anyone else in the apartment that night?' he queried. 'Wishart's wife, for instance?'

'Nope. She's been in her grave the past four years. The only other person present at that time, far as I could gather, was Dan Meeker, Wishart's bank guard, who's always on duty in the apartment as a general runabout when there's game on; serves the players drinks and the like. I got a statement from him. He rushed down to the bank before the gun echoes had faded, and found Wishart lying dead in front of the open safe and the back door wide open. Meeker is an all-right guy. I'd trust him with my life.'

Morgan added Meeker's name to his list and got to his feet. 'If that's all you can tell me then I'd better start doing my job,' he said. 'I'll be dropping in on you from time to time, keeping you up to date with my progress. Now I better take a look around town before I start checking out the witnesses. I'll report to you daily, unless I'm out of town.'

'I wish you luck. You're gonna need it.' Cassidy did not sound confident. 'Let me know when you come up against that brick wall, huh?'

Morgan smiled and left the office. He looked around, thinking about the HW outfit, and walked his horse along the street to a large building that looked like a hotel. He hitched the animal to a rail and went in, carrying his saddle-bags, and the clerk behind the desk eyed him suspiciously, running an experienced eye over Morgan's big figure and dusty appearance.

33

'I'll need a room for about a week,' Morgan said. The clerk spun the register for him to sign, then quickly turned it back to scrutinize the signature.

'May I ask what your business is in town, mister?'

'Sure. You can ask.' Morgan looked into the man's narrowed eyes and did not like the long, thin face, which reminded him of a weasel.

The clerk squirmed at Morgan's sharp tone. 'I was thinking I could maybe point you in the right direction if I knew who you're here to see,' he said quickly. 'No offence offered, mister. It's just that I know everyone in town and mebbe I could help you.'

'No offence taken. Give me the key.' Morgan held out a large hand and the clerk turned to take a key off a board on the wall behind the desk and dropped it into the hand. 'Thanks. Where's the room?'

'Up the stairs to the left. Number Nine.'

Morgan went to the stairs and ascended swiftly. He glanced back down at the lobby when he reached the landing and saw the clerk scuttling towards the street door like a scared rabbit. He turned quickly, descended to the lobby again and walked out to the sidewalk to look around. He was in time to see the clerk hurrying to an office along to thc left, where he paused to look around furtively before disappearing inside.

Shrugging, Morgan went back into the hotel and ascended to his room. He dumped his saddle-bags on the bed and crossed to the window, which overlooked the street, thrusting it open to lean out and look around. He saw the hotel clerk emerging from the office. The man paused to look around and then came hurrying back to the hotel. Morgan saw a sign outside the office which read JONAS DRAPER ATTORNEY-AT-LAW. He watched the clerk's return until the man disappeared into the lobby, then closed the window and left the room, deciding that it was time to take care of his horse.

Down in the lobby, Morgan confronted the clerk.

'What's your name?' he asked.

'Amos Henty, at your service, sir.'

'Why did you run along to Draper's office to report my presence in town? Was it me in particular, or do you report the arrival of every stranger to the lawyer?'

Henty's face lost its colour. He shook his head. 'It ain't what you're thinking, Mr Morgan. Jonas Draper owns the hotel. If he wants a run-down on every stranger who books in then I can't deny him. If I don't do like he says I'd lose my job.'

'Is Draper on the town council?'

'He sure is. He's in the big saddle around here.'

'So he'd know a Pinkerton man has been sent for,' Morgan mused. 'That figures. I'll be seeing Draper shortly.'

He left the hotel and swung into his

saddle, riding to the left towards the livery barn. As he passed Draper's office he saw a small man wearing a store suit standing in the doorway. He lifted a hand to his hatbrim in a mock salute. The man turned abruptly and disappeared into the office.

Morgan continued to the stable. He dismounted outside and permitted the horse to drink from the conveniently placed water trough, his gaze roving around the street as he waited for the animal to take its fill. A sound attracted his attention and he looked towards the big stable doorway to see a man staggering out of the dim interior, bent over and whimpering in a choked tone. Morgan's initial thought was that the man was drunk, then saw blood showing on his shirt and the handle of a knife protruding from his chest. The man collapsed face down in the dust, and Morgan knew by the way he had fallen that he was dead.

Acting instinctively, Morgan leapt over the body and ran into the stable, drawing his gun as he moved. He paused inside the doorway, gun swinging as he covered the interior. The stable was silent and still. There was no sign of a struggle or an assailant. The big back door was wide open and he heard no sign of departure in that direction. He walked the length of the long barn, checking the stalls until he reached the back door, and when he peered out over the back lots he saw no sign of life. The silence was chilling, and he turned abruptly and went back to the dead man.

Morgan turned the man over, taking in physical details. Aged about forty, his angular face showing the grey sheen of death beneath its dark tan, the dead man was dressed in a brown store suit and dusty shoes. His face was clean-shaven, his hair almost white in the glaring afternoon sun, and his half-open blue eyes were fixed in a glazing stare into the mouth of hell.

A boot scraped behind Morgan. He

arose and turned in one lithe movement, like a cougar ready to protect its
cubs. His right hand moved in a blur of
speed and his gun appeared, clutched
in his fist, lining up on the tall man who
had paused in the doorway of the barn.
A deputy's badge glinted on the
newcomer's shirt front. His right hand
was down on the butt of the gun
holstered on his right hip but he
remained immobile, his mouth agape in
shock, due to Morgan's lightning-speed
draw and the sight of the dead man
lying in the dust.

'What's going on here?' the deputy
demanded.

'Where were you a couple of minutes
ago?' Morgan countered.

'I came along the back lots and
turned in at the rear door.' The deputy
was fighting against shock. He pointed
at the corpse. 'Who is he, and who
killed him?'

'I was hoping you could tell me.'
Morgan holstered his gun with practised ease. He noted several pieces of

straw sticking to the deputy's shirt. 'I was watering my horse when this guy came staggering out of the barn and flopped into the dust. I checked the stable, and looked out the back door, but there was no one around — not even you. Where did you spring from?'

'I'm Mike Bradley.' The deputy's voice hesitated slightly before continuing. 'I was handling some personal business in the dress shop. Who are you, mister? What's going on? Two strangers in town — one dead and the other standing over him. Is that your knife in his chest?'

'I'm Cleef Morgan from Pinkerton's. I don't carry a knife. As for your business in the dress shop, I suspect you were up in the hay loft when this man was stabbed.'

Bradley's jaw dropped and he moistened his lips. Then he nodded slowly. 'You are some detective,' he observed. 'But if I came from the dress shop or out of the loft doesn't matter. I'd like to know where the killer went — unless this guy stabbed himself!'

'Which is unlikely.' Morgan smiled briefly but his eyes were filled with a cold, hard expression. 'I reckon it's more likely you stabbed him and went up into the hayloft when you heard my horse approaching.'

'Me!' Bradley shook his head and stepped backwards into the doorway of the barn. 'Hey, Mattie,' he called. 'Come on out here.'

Morgan waited stolidly, his eyes narrowing when he heard sounds inside the stable, and a few moments later a tall, slim, dark-haired girl of about twenty appeared in the doorway of the barn, her attractive face expressing concern. She was wearing a low-cut red dress and sandals on her bare feet. Her gaze was drawn immediately to the dead man and she gasped and lifted a hand to her mouth, her eyes widening as shock hit her. She fell back a step and uttered a faint cry of horror.

'This is Mattie Scarfe,' Bradley said heavily. 'We were up in the hayloft together, and I'd like that fact kept quiet. I'm telling you so you won't harbour suspicions about me.' He looked at the girl. 'This is Morgan, the Pinkerton detective we've been expecting.'

'I'm satisfied, for the moment.' Morgan's eyes were on the girl, and he saw her confusion grow when she learned his identity. 'Do you know the dead man?' he enquired.

She shook her head mutely. Her mouth opened convulsively but she was unable to speak. She pressed the back of a hand tightly against her lips and closed her eyes.

'I can tell you he's a stranger around here,' Bradley said sharply. 'Have you spoken to the sheriff yet?'

'First thing I did when I hit town.' Morgan did not take his eyes off the girl. 'How did this man get into town? Someone must have seen his arrival? Did he get off a stagecoach? He looks the type who would travel that way.'

'I'll see if he rented a room at the

hotel.' Bradley patted the girl's shoulder. 'Run along now, Mattie. I'll see you later. Go out the back way and along the alley so you're not seen.'

The girl took a last look at the corpse and faded back into the shadows in the barn. It was in Morgan's mind to call her back, but she seemed inhibited by Bradley's presence and he thought she would be more forthcoming when the deputy was not around. He'd gained the impression that the dead man was not a stranger to her. She had been shocked by the sight of the man on the ground but not surprised.

'Is she a married woman?' Morgan asked.

'Why do you ask that?' A frown settled on Bradley's face. 'You'd do better to forget Mattie was here.'

'You're taking trouble to ensure secrecy. That's usually a sign that those involved in such meetings are not supposed to be seeing one another.'

Bradley shook his head. 'It's nothing like that. Mattie's pa, Bill Scarfe, doesn't approve of his only daughter seeing a lawman. He wants her to marry Buck Whiteman, the no-good son of Hank Whiteman, who owns the HW ranch. Between them, the Whitemans think they own this country, and maybe they do. But Mattie won't marry Buck if I have anything to do with it. That no-good has been showing an interest in her for some time now, and I think he's turning her head with his attentions.'

'Did you hear the HW outfit ride out of town a short time ago, firing their guns?'

'I'd have to be dead not to.' Bradley's face twisted into anger. 'I was skulking up in the loft, watching them. On the sheriff's orders, you understand.'

Morgan nodded. 'You'd better report this murder to the sheriff pronto,' he advised. 'In the meantime, I'll take care of my horse.'

Bradley moved off immediately, striding along the street, and Morgan grasped his reins and led the brown stallion away from the trough. He took the animal into the barn and put it into a stall. A moment later Mattie Scarfe appeared at his side, and he paused in unsaddling the horse and smiled at her.

'I figured you'd want to tell me what's on your mind,' he mused.

'How do you know that?' she countered in surprise.

'I couldn't explain. It's just a knack that comes from experience and observation.' Morgan smiled as he picked a piece of straw from the shoulder of the girl's dress, and her cheeks reddened when she saw it.

'I hope you won't have to tell anyone that you saw me here with Mike,' she said worriedly. 'It's my father, you see. He runs Ashby's saloon and reckons I'm too good to be a lawman's wife.' She paused uncertainly, and her voice faltered when she continued. 'The trouble is, Pa has a drinking problem although he won't admit it, and he's threatened to take a gun to Mike if I don't stop seeing him.'

'My lips are sealed,' Morgan said. 'I've already forgotten that I saw you here.'

'Thank you.' Relief sounded in her voice and she turned to slip away.

'Just a moment.' He spoke quickly, and she paused like a startled fawn. 'I sensed that you recognized the dead man when you saw him. It was something that showed in your eyes for a split second. Mike is denying all knowledge of the man's identity, so if you can put a name to the murder victim I'd be mighty appreciative, and then nothing this side of Boot Hill would drag the fact from me that I saw you here with Mike.'

Her face underwent a series of rapidly changing emotions as she gazed at him, and finally showed resignation. She sighed deeply and then reached out and grasped his sleeve.

'That's blackmail!' she gasped, and when he remained silently gazing at her she went on hesitantly, 'All I know is that his name is Cass Frayne. I overheard my father talking to Sam Ashby. I've taken to eavesdropping on my father because I was afraid that when he's had too much to drink he might try to do some harm to Mike.'

Her voice trailed off and she gazed imploringly at Morgan, who still remained silent, and after a few moments she moistened her lips and continued.

'Frayne was a gunslinger whom Ashby brought in to safeguard his interests, and was kept strictly in the background. During the day Frayne never stirred from his room in Ashby's house, and the Lord knows what he did at night. I don't think anyone saw him around town. He was like a shadow. I don't know what he was doing for Ashby, but he departed about a month ago, and I'd forgotten about him until I saw him lying dead outside.'

'So that was why you were so shocked when you saw him.' Morgan nodded. 'But you must have seen Frayne somewhere to be able to recognize him. Tell me about that.'

'Frayne came regularly into a private room at the saloon for a drink, and I used to serve him. He never ever spoke to me. I also heard Jonas Draper, the lawyer, mention Frayne to my father, so some men in town knew about him.'

'What you've told me is very interesting.' Morgan patted Mattie's arm. 'I won't tell anyone I saw you here in the stable if you forget what you've just told me. Is it a deal?'

She nodded dumbly, then turned and hurried away, leaving by the back door. Morgan was thoughtful as he tended his horse, and when he was through he left the stable and walked along the street to Ashby's saloon. Pausing at the batwings, he looked around the street and saw the sheriff and the deputy emerging from the law office to come hurrying towards the stable. He shook his head and entered the saloon, not wanting to get further involved with the death of Cass Frayne.

The saloon was a large square room

with a bar running along the right-hand side and gaming tables occupying the centre space. A flight of stairs at the far end led up to living-quarters. There were only two customers at this time of the afternoon, and Morgan gave his attention to the tall, thin man standing behind the bar. He could tell at a glance that this was Mattie Scarfe's father, for the resemblance between the two was uncanny. Scarfe was middle-aged, with a pock-marked face and bleary eyes. He was thin, looking as if he did not enjoy good health, and when he gazed at Morgan his blue eyes seemed unfocused.

'Howdy, stranger,' Scarfe greeted in a mock jovial tone. 'What'll be?'

'Beer,' Morgan replied, and slapped a silver coin on the polished bar. He waited stolidly until a foaming glass was placed before him, aware that Scarfe was subjecting him to a close scrutiny. 'I'm Cleef Morgan,' he said suddenly. 'I'm a Pinkerton detective, and you can guess at the reason for my arrival.'

'Is that a fact?' Scarfe did not seem inordinately interested. 'It's a good thing you didn't show a little earlier. You would have walked into the middle of the HW outfit, and they ain't too happy with lawmen at this time.'

'They'll get their chance,' Morgan responded with a faint smile. 'I shall be riding out to the HW ranch soon as I can make it.'

'You're here to check out Wishart's murder and the bank robbery, huh?' Scarfe leaned his elbows on the bar. He was breathing heavily, his breath wheezing deep in his chest. 'I don't know why they sent for you. It's a clear case, and don't need a detective sticking his nose in. Gus Mulder made big tracks around this county for a lot of years, and mebbe thought he could get away with murder and robbery. But there are folks around who won't stand for that kind of behaviour, and if Mulder is ever caught he's likely to find rough justice in the shape of a lynch mob. I've heard strong talk about it in here, and what's

50

said while men are drinking is usually straight stuff.'

'Thanks for the information.' Morgan drained his glass and smacked his lips. 'I needed that. See you around.'

He turned abruptly and walked to the batwings, his spurs jingling. He thrust open the swing doors, then paused, for two men appeared on the sidewalk, stepping forward from either side of the doorway, and one of them jabbed the hard muzzle of a pistol against his belly.

3

Morgan froze with the gun muzzle digging into his stomach. He looked at the face of the man holding the gun and saw deadly intention in slitted brown eyes. The second man reached out a hand and dragged Morgan's pistol from its holster.

'What's this — a hold-up?' Morgan demanded. 'In broad daylight, too. You're making a big mistake, gents. I'm flat broke. Was about to ride out to one of the ranches for a job.'

'You ain't no cowhand,' rasped the man with the gun. 'I saw you come in here. You're that damn detective about to stick your nose into business we aim to handle. We're gonna run you outa town, mister, and you'll make a big mistake if you come back. Now head for the stable. We'll pick up your hoss and set you on your way. We got plans for the reward being offered for getting back the bank's money, and we've already put in a lot of time and effort trying to get a line on Gus Mulder. No johnny-come-lately is gonna muscle in on our game.'

'Who told you I'm a detective?' Morgan was already listing in his mind the people in town who knew his identity, and he instinctively thought of Amos Henty, the hotel clerk. He tried a shot in the dark. 'Henty ain't the kind of man I'd rely on for information,' he said.

'Who said anything about Henty?' The gun muzzle bored harder into Morgan's side. 'What are you trying to pull, mister? You're asking for a bullet where you can't digest it. Get moving. Go left and into the alley. Make for the back lots, and we'll send you off in style. But if you come back you'll collect a slug right where my gun is boring you.'

Morgan shrugged and moved obediently to his left while the two men half-turned to fall in behind him. For a split second neither of the guns directed at him had a clear shot, and Morgan spun quickly, stepping to his right and leaning in as his big left fist sledged up in a powerful hook to crack against the jaw of the nearest man. The man's legs buckled. Morgan snatched the gun and presented the muzzle at the chest of the second man, who tried desperately to swing the pistol he had taken from Morgan. Realizing that he would be too late to stop the man from shooting, Morgan fired, aiming for the man's right shoulder.

The thunderclap of the shot threw echoes across the silent town. Morgan restrained his breathing as gunsmoke flared around him. He struck out with the pistol as the man staggered under the smashing impact of the heavy slug, and the muzzle struck the man's gun wrist. The pistol fell to the ground and the man cried out in pain as he pitched over sideways to the dusty sidewalk.

The first man was trying to get to his

feet, his senses scrambled by Morgan's fist, but he had pulled a knife and was intent on using it. Morgan kicked out shrewdly with his right toe, connecting with the man's hand. The knife flew in an arc, glinting in the sunlight, and landed in the dust of the street. Morgan kicked again, and this time his toe thudded against the man's chin. He bent and retrieved his gun from the sidewalk and then stepped back to review the situation. Both men were unconscious.

Morgan looked around the street. The shot had not alerted anyone. Then he saw the sheriff and the deputy emerging from the livery barn. They paused to look around before running towards him. Morgan checked his gun and returned it to his holster. He bent and disarmed the man who had held him up. Checking the second man, he saw that the shot had struck him in the upper chest. Blood was leaking from the wound. The man's face was pale and he was semi-conscious.

Cassidy and Bradley arrived. The sheriff was breathing heavily, his face twisted with the effort of running. Bradley demanded to know what had happened while the sheriff leaned against the wall of the saloon to recover from his exertions. Morgan explained the situation, then handed over the guns he had taken from the men.

'Lock them up,' he said. 'There are a couple of other men I need to see in a hurry. I'll come to these when I get through.'

'Is this the way you operate?' Cassidy wheezed as his breathing returned to normal. 'It ain't how we do things around here, Morgan. You can't ride rough-shod over folks.'

'Mebbe your tactics are wrong,' Morgan suggested. 'I reckon that's why you had to send to Pinkerton for help. Listen, Sheriff, and get this good. You can tell me what you want done, but you don't tell me how to do it.'

He turned and went across the street, ignoring the sheriff's order to remain.

Men were appearing on the street, looking around curiously for the source of the shot. Morgan saw the small figure of the lawyer standing in the doorway of his office, and his eyes glinted when the man turned quickly and hurried inside. Morgan reached the door of the office in time to hear a key being turned in the lock.

Without hesitation he raised his right foot and kicked the door powerfully, using all of his considerable weight. The lock gave way and the door flew inwards, narrowly missing the man standing inside the office. Morgan caught the door on the rebound, his gaze fixed upon the paling face of the cowering man.

'So tell me what is going on,' Morgan commanded.

'Are you loco? Who are you? Why have you broken my door?'

'I'm guessing you're Draper, the attorney. Correct?'

'Yes. I'm Jonas Draper.'

'You obviously know who I am. Your

57

hotel clerk almost busted a gut getting here to tell you I'd arrived after I'd booked in. So loosen up, mister. Two men accosted me when I left the saloon. They knew my identity and planned to run me out of town. You set them on me and I want to know why.'

Jonas Draper was several inches shorter than six feet. Dressed in a light-blue suit, white shirt and a vest that matched his suit, he wore a black string tie around his thin neck, and flinched when Morgan reached out and grasped the tie in an unbreakable grip.

'What are you doing?' he gasped. 'Get your hand off me. I'll report you to the sheriff if you're not careful.'

'Let's go talk to the sheriff now.' Morgan took hold of Draper's arm and started across the street towards the front of the saloon, where a crowd was gathering around the two lawmen and the hardcases.

'Wait.' Draper spoke desperately. 'Come into my office and we'll talk. I never sent those men to attack you. I knew about them, but it was not my idea.'

'Then whose idea was it?' Morgan turned back to the office, still holding the lawyer's arm. They entered, and Morgan kicked the door to with his heel. He released the lawyer and stood watching him closely.

'You can't handle me like this,' Draper protested. 'It's against the law, and you're supposed to be working for the law.'

'So report me to the sheriff when I get through — if there's anything left of you by that time.' Morgan grinned. 'Lie to me and I'll get really rough, and I know enough about this business to recognize lies when I hear them.'

'I didn't set those two men on you.' Draper tried to loosen his tie, which had pulled tight under Morgan's grip.

'Forget those two. I wanta know exactly what happened the night the bank got robbed and Wishart was shot dead.'

Draper was startled by the unexpected change of subject. He caught his breath and his eyes filled with wariness. He turned abruptly, went to the desk and sat down heavily on the seat behind it, his gaze not leaving Morgan's face.

'And stick to the facts,' Morgan reminded.

'I made a statement to the sheriff immediately after the incident.'

'I want to hear your version now, so get to it.' Morgan produced his notebook.

'There's nothing much to tell. We all met in Wishart's apartment like we'd done for months. It was a regular event. There were five of us as usual. It was no different from any other time.'

'So Mulder got Wishart to take him down into the bank every Saturday night to make a withdrawal, huh?'

'No. Of course not. It was the first time that happened.'

'Then why say that particular night was no different from any other? You're not telling it as it happened, mister. Why did Mulder insist on having cash at that time of the night? The game was a regular thing, so he would have ensured that he had sufficient stakes. And in a game like that — all local businessmen — the others would have accepted a note, huh? Mulder's credit was good, wasn't it?'

'Sure, but that particular evening Whiteman was needling Mulder from the start. The two of them were at loggerheads over water rights, but there was always some bad feeling between them. Whiteman is that type of man. He likes to twist the knife in a wound.'

'So Whiteman forced the issue that night?'

'Mulder didn't have much cash. He hadn't been able to get into town before the game, and Whiteman made a big thing about taking an IOU, although he had never objected before. Mulder was an honourable man who always paid his debts, and sometimes he was a big loser. He liked to think he was the world's best poker-player, but was rash most of the time. He drinking heavily that evening, too, I remember, and became aggressive, although that was not his normal character. When Whiteman questioned an IOU, Mulder turned on Wishart and demanded cash. Wishart didn't want to go down to the bank after closing time and offered some of his cash against a personal IOU, but Mulder wouldn't have it. He wanted his own money, and to stop the deterioration of the game, Wishart took him down into the bank.'

'So Whiteman brought about the situation. His attitude to Mulder was the reason why Wishart and Mulder went down to the bank.'

Draper shook his head doubtfully but did not reply.

'That's what you said,' Morgan rapped. 'Is that the way it happened or wasn't it?'

'That's it exactly,' Draper admitted reluctantly.

'And did you report that fact in your statement to the sheriff?'

Draper squirmed in his seat. He looked uncomfortable, clenching and unclenching his hands. Again he shook his head, clearly disliking the slant of Morgan's questions.

'Yes or no,' Morgan demanded. 'Did you report that fact to the sheriff?'

'I didn't.' Draper sighed heavily and beads of perspiration broke out on his forehead.

'Why not? As a lawyer you must have realized it was a vital piece of evidence. If Mulder hadn't been baited by Whiteman he wouldn't have insisted on withdrawing money from the bank and the robbery and killing couldn't have occurred. So I ask myself if the whole business was planned to happen the way it did, and not by Mulder.'

'Then by whom?' Draper was frowning. 'The men who were present are solid, law-abiding businessmen. We've all known each other for years.'

'Mulder was one of you, yet he's disappeared, and it looks as if he killed Wishart and got away with twenty thousand dollars.' Morgan shook his head. 'What do you think happened that night? We know what everyone thinks happened. But you were on the inside. So how did you read it with your legally trained mind?'

'I've got no idea. I didn't know what was going on. I was surprised by Whiteman's attitude, although he and Mulder were never on real friendly terms. But I didn't get the impression that anything special was happening. We were all genuinely shocked when the shots were fired. Dan Meeker was the first to recover from the shock. He dashed down to the bank and found the back door open, Wishart dead, and Mulder and twenty thousand dollars missing. I think there can be no doubt of Mulder's guilt. He disappeared that night and hasn't been seen since.'

'That could be because someone made it look like he did it,' Morgan mused. 'He might have been killed the same time Wishart was. There were two shots, weren't there?' He wrote a reminder in his notebook to see the report of the doctor's examination of

Wishart's body. 'When the sheriff gave me the facts of this case I thought it was obvious what had happened — which is the popular view. But you've thrown an entirely different light on it, and now I'm not so sure. I'll be coming back to you, Draper, so hold yourself ready for more questions. And if I get any more interference from you I'll come down pretty hard on you.'

He heard the lawyer heave a big sigh of relief as he turned to depart, but then he swung round and confronted Draper again. The lawyer seemed to shrink back into his seat.

'Before I leave, tell me about the two hardcases who accosted me outside the saloon,' Morgan rasped. 'You said you didn't send them after me, but hinted you knew who did.'

'I don't know who set them on you.' Draper shook his head emphatically.

Morgan took a pace towards the desk, scaring Draper immensely, and then changed his mind and departed, mulling over what he had learned. The crowd standing in front of Ashby's saloon had grown considerably, and he saw Mike Bradley escorting the uninjured hardcase along the opposite sidewalk to the jail. Sheriff Cassidy was standing beside the man Morgan had shot, now lying inertly on his back with a man tending his wound.

Hoofbeats sounded from along the street and Morgan narrowed his eyes when he saw three riders coming into town at a fast clip. The foremost of the trio was a girl — no more than twenty or so, he thought. She was astride a powerful grey horse that seemed difficult to ride. Dressed in good range clothes, she presented an attractive picture — her oval face framed by golden curls beneath a flat-brimmed Plains hat.

Morgan started across the street as the girl and her companions reined up on the edge of the crowd. He saw Cassidy look round and then walk towards the newcomers, reaching out to grasp the girl's bridle as she dismounted. As he drew nearer, Morgan was intrigued by the girl's features. She was good to look upon, and the stormy determination stamped on her features enhanced her beauty. Her well-fitting blue pants and beige vest could not conceal the attractive lines of her slender figure. As he drew near to her his size forced itself upon her awareness and she glanced up at him, her blue eyes fringed by long lashes, instantly charming him with the warmth of her strong personality. She was talking to the sheriff, but Morgan's arrival made some kind of impact upon her for she fell silent and gazed at him speculatively, eyeing with interest the holstered gun on his right hip.

Cassidy glanced at him, nodded, and said to the girl from a corner of his mouth:

'Jenny, meet Cleef Morgan, the Pinkerton detective I sent for. Morgan, this is Jenny Mulder. She's bossing Big G in her father's absence.'

The expression which came to the girl's face would have withered a lesser man but Morgan merely shrugged his wide shoulders. He smiled disarmingly.

'How do you do, Miss Mulder,' he greeted.

'How do you think I'm doing?' she demanded, and Morgan noted that she was under great stress. 'My father has disappeared and is accused of robbery and murder. I am at my wit's end trying to run the ranch in his absence, and I have trouble on the range that multiplies daily.'

'You have my sympathy.' Morgan's tone was gentle. 'I can understand your feelings. This must have been a terrible shock for you. Have you had no word of your father since his disappearance?'

Her expression hardened and she shook her head. 'It's as if he's disappeared from the face of the earth. I don't know if he is alive or dead. And everyone has judged him guilty of what happened when the bank was robbed. I hope you will be able to throw some light on that dreadful night.' She returned her attention to Cassidy.

'That's why I've come to town. Have you discovered anything yet, Sheriff? I can't go on like this much longer, not knowing the truth.'

'I'm real sorry, Jenny.' Cassidy shook his head. 'Nothing's come up since I saw you last. It's all a big mystery to me. I don't know what to think any more. But I've got my hopes pinned on Morgan. He's got a sizeable reputation, and I feel sure he'll soon turn up something.'

'I'd like to have a talk with you, Mr Morgan,' the girl said.

'I certainly want to talk to you,' he responded. 'Will you be in town long? I need to speak with the doctor before I go any further.'

'I shall be at the hotel. Perhaps you'll come to me there.' She turned away, handed her reins to one of the riders who had accompanied her into town, and both men wheeled their mounts and rode along to the stable. The girl walked towards the hotel.

Morgan moved to the shoulder of the

tall man on his knees beside the wounded hard case, bandaging the man's wound. The sheriff remained at his side.

'Doc,' Cassidy said. 'This is Cleef Morgan, the Pinkerton man. He shot this jasper.'

The doctor looked up and nodded. 'Glad to know you, Morgan. I'm Bill Caylin. I'm just about through here. I'll talk to you in a minute.'

'No hurry,' Morgan replied. He turned his attention to the sheriff. 'What can you tell me about these two men who accosted me? Do they work for anyone in town?'

'They rode in last night, and as they seemed to have plenty of dough I didn't bother them.'

'So they're strangers.'

'Yep. Ain't seen either of them before.'

'And yet they knew all about me,' Morgan mused. 'That ain't so good. I figured Draper set them on me, but I ain't sure.'

'Draper!' The sheriff gazed at Morgan in surprise. 'What put you on to him? He's the town lawyer, after all's said and done.'

Morgan explained his chat with the lawyer, and Cassidy shook his head.

'I know for a fact that there's been bad blood between Mulder and Whiteman for a long time, but it puts the proceedings of that night the bank was robbed in a different light if Whiteman did needle Mulder into demanding cash from his account. Heck, it could almost point to Mulder being a victim instead of the killer.'

'Let it rest for now,' Morgan advised. 'You've handed the investigation over to me and I want to conduct it as I see fit.'

'With pleasure.' Cassidy nodded eagerly. 'I'm sure out of my depth with it.'

'Two shots were fired when Wishart was killed in the bank, huh?'

'Sure thing. Everyone remembers two shots.'

'So how was Wishart killed?'

'A single shot between the eyes.' Cassidy frowned. 'What are you getting at?'

'Just testing the evidence.' Morgan smiled. 'Did you check the inside of the bank to find where the slugs finished up?'

'Hell no! The doc found one in Wishart, but I don't know what happened to the second one.'

'What calibre bullet killed Wishart?'

'A hideout gun was used. It was a .41 slug.'

'Was Mulder carrying a gun that night?'

'None of them was. But Mulder could have had a derringer in his pocket and no one would have been any the wiser.'

Morgan nodded. 'Check out the bank and see if that second slug is lodged in a wall. Were there any bloodstains apart from Wishart's?'

'Nope. If Mulder was shot there then he didn't bleed. I was in the bank within minutes of the shooting and had a good look around. I've got to say that I go along with the evidence as I see it, so I don't believe Mulder was shot and removed from the scene before the rest of the cardplayers got down there. There was no time for that. Dan Meeker, the bank guard, ran down to the bank instantly, certainly within a minute of hearing the shots, and all he found was Wishart dead in front of the open safe and Mulder and the money gone. The back door of the bank was wide open and Meeker checked outside. He didn't see anyone around, and later I asked around town for witnesses, but didn't find a soul who admitted to being in the area at that time.'

Morgan considered what he had assimilated. But he was maintaining an open mind. 'I'll get round to talking to the other card-players before I do anything else,' he said, 'and if they're like Draper they'll change their stories when I question them. What can you tell me about the trouble between Whiteman and Mulder? I assume they are neighbours on the range.'

Cassidy heaved a sigh and shook his head. 'It's all over nothing,' he said. 'Whiteman says Mulder, whose spread is north of HW, plans to dam the stream that runs across both their ranges, which would leave HW high and dry. Mulder has always denied it, and hasn't done anything about it in five years. But that don't cut no ice with Whiteman. Between you and me, I reckon Whiteman is using the water question as an excuse to make trouble. I sure didn't find anything wrong when I took a look around the range. But there it is. The story has never died, and Whiteman is on the prod because of it.'

'What other trouble have you got in the county?' There were traces of impatience in Morgan's voice.

Cassidy shook his head. 'Nothing much. A bit of rustling. The usual thing. But Whiteman ran off some nesters a couple of months ago, and killed two men in the process. He proved it was self-defence. I reckon that's why he's got night riders hitting his range now. The surviving nesters were mighty stirred up by the shooting. Some of them have settled in town, and I've heard whispers that they're planning to get even with HW.'

'And Whiteman buried one of his riders this afternoon, who was killed by a night rider. Looks like that trouble is beginning to hot up.'

Cassidy heaved a sigh, then smiled, and relief suffused his craggy face. 'Yeah, it sure looks like it, but your arrival has taken a big weight off my shoulders.'

'I'm going to talk to Jenny Mulder now.' Morgan was thoughtful for a moment, considering what he had learned. 'There's one thing about this business that really bothers me. Would Mulder, if he's guilty, kill Wishart and rob the bank on the spur of the moment and then just disappear like that? What about his daughter? He would know how she'd suffer. Would he put her through such agony?'

'That's what I can't figure.' Cassidy frowned. 'Knowing Mulder as I do, I'd stake my life on him. He loved that girl of his. She was the apple of his eye. He wouldn't dream of doing such a thing to her. And for many years he was staunchly law-biding. I never knew him to put a foot wrong. It wasn't in him. That's why what happened is so shocking.'

Morgan nodded. 'You talk as if you know Mulder is dead,' he observed.

Cassidy shrugged and shook his head. 'That's how it looks to me,' he replied.

'I'll check with you later.' Morgan turned away. 'I'll drop by your office. I need to look at a map of the county so I can find my way around. See you later.'

He took his leave of the sheriff and walked towards the hotel, eager to see Jenny Mulder again and needing some background information on her father. Pausing in front of the hotel at the sound of approaching hoofs, he turned to watch three riders coming along the street. The foremost was a powerful man in his middle forties, riding a big buckskin, his heavy features almost concealed by the wide brim of a black Stetson. He was massively built, and brute strength was evident in every line of his bulky figure. Large hands were clenched around his reins and, spotting Morgan, he yanked the head of his horse around roughly and came to the edge of the sidewalk where the detective was standing. He reined in, stepped down from his high saddle and handed his reins to one of the two hard-bitten men accompanying him, his every movement emphasizing arrogance.

'Stable him,' he rasped. 'I'll be staying in town until I've seen the Mulder gal. It's time our problems were settled.' He turned and looked at Morgan, standing almost as tall, but outweighing the detective by many pounds. 'You're a stranger round here,' he growled. 'Who in hell are you? Not that detective feller Cassidy is waiting for, are you?'

'I am,' Morgan replied. 'Who are you?'

'Hank Whiteman. I own the HW ranch. So you're what a detective looks like, huh? Well, I reckon Cassidy is wasting his time. There's been too much water under the bridge since Mulder killed Wishart and made off with the bank money. You ain't gonna prove anything, mister, and if you had any sense you'd give it best and pull out before you get too involved.'

'And I'm glad to meet you, Whiteman,' Morgan responded. 'You've saved me a trip out to your place. I need to go over your statement with you about the incidents that occurred the night Wishart was killed.'

Whiteman laughed boisterously and shook his head. 'Leave me out of your fun and games,' he said fiercely. 'I told Cassidy all I know. I ain't got time to chow over past events.' He thrust out his prominent chin. 'And you ain't big enough to make me do what I ain't got a mind to. As far as I'm concerned, you ain't even a proper lawman.' He slapped his thigh and laughed uproariously.

Morgan stepped down off the sidewalk and the big rancher fell back a step, his brown eyes narrowing as he tried to gauge the next move. Morgan's left foot slid forward a half-pace as he unleashed his left fist in a tremendous hook that exploded against Whiteman's jaw. The rancher bellowed as he went over backwards to land on his shoulders in the dust, and then came surging upright, his eyes filled with passion, like those of a wild bull, his fists clenched and swinging.

4

Whiteman lunged at Morgan, head drawn down into his powerful shoulders, his eyes like two flames in his rugged face. Hamlike fists, held shoulder-high, described tiny circles as he lunged in. He loosed a left-hand swing that would have torn off Morgan's head, but before it connected a jarring punch exploded like a pistol shot against his jaw. His balance seemed to go haywire as he was carried backwards on scrabbling feet under the impact, and Morgan followed him up like a preying cougar. Whiteman shook his head and quickly recovered his balance, a wariness showing in his narrowed eyes as he resumed his guard. He advanced quickly, steadying himself as he prepared to hammer Morgan into the dust.

But Morgan was not fighting for pleasure. His intention was to knock some respect for the law into White-man's thick head. His right fist, knotty and seemingly iron-bound, flashed out and again connected with Whiteman's jaw. The vicious crack of the blow rang in Whiteman's ears and pain stabbed through his head and down the nerves in his neck. He reeled backwards again, and suddenly found himself on his knees in the dust and not knowing how he got there. He shook his head to clear his whirling senses and looked up at Morgan, who was standing over him with fists cocked and an infuriating grin on his hard-expressioned face.

'If you've a mind to try again then get up,' Morgan rasped. 'All I wanta do is get some answers from you. I don't like your disrespect for the law, Whiteman, and I've a mind to pound some sense into your skull. Before you go any further, I want to tell you that apart from being a Pinkerton detective, I'm also a US deputy marshal, and if you refuse to answer my questions I'll throw you in the hoosegow until hell freezes over.'

Whiteman lunged to his feet, but staggered as his senses reeled. He dropped back into the dust on his hands and knees, shaking his head as he tried to work out what had happened. Again he tried to look up at Morgan but his head sagged forward and he was filled with a great reluctance to absorb more punishment. He got to one knee. Morgan reached out his left hand and grasped the rancher's upper arm to help him to his feet, supporting him until he had recovered his equilibrium.

'You had enough?' Morgan demanded. 'I'd rather ask questions than fight. But if you've a mind to carry on then I'll accommodate you.'

'I've had enough for now,' Whiteman growled. 'What in hell do you eat for breakfast, fighting like that?'

Morgan grinned. 'Sounds like you're ready to answer some questions now. I could do with a beer. What about you? You sounded like you don't like lawmen, but I'll buy you a drink if you're willing to forgo the rough stuff and answer my questions like a law-abiding man.'

'It's a deal. I've been expecting you to show up for the past two weeks. What took you so long?'

'Ever heard of Scrag Hanton.'

'Yeah. Hasn't everybody? He was killed last week. Say, was it you nailed him?'

'I met up with him over by Juniper Bend.'

'That says it all.' Whiteman shook his head. 'You got my respect, mister. What questions do you wanta ask? My legs feel like they don't belong to me so I'll sit down on the edge of the sidewalk while you fire away. You wanta know what happened the night Wishart was killed, huh?'

'I'm more interested in the men who were playing cards that night,' Morgan said. 'I heard that you and Mulder didn't get along very well. What was the trouble between you?'

'The worst kind of trouble a rancher

can have.' Whiteman felt his jaw gingerly. 'You pack an almighty powerful punch, Morgan — like the kick of a mule. Water rights. That's the key to the problem. Mulder was going to dam my main source of water, and no rancher worth his salt will stand for that. My herd would die of thirst. Hell, never tell a rancher you're gonna cut him off from his water supply unless you're tired of living.'

'Mulder might have said he'd do it, but he didn't make a move in that direction, did he? How did that rumour crop up?'

'I don't know. I sure didn't dream it, and he never denied it when I confronted him. But if Mulder said he would do it then one day I knew I'd wake up and find it done. I wasn't prepared to wait until it was too late so I needled Mulder every chance I got, to push him into doing it or turning away from the idea.'

'Why did Mulder threaten to stop your water in the first place?'

'I guess he didn't like the kind of tracks I make around here.' Whiteman grunted painfully as he settled himself on the edge of the sidewalk. 'Hell, I know I'm a damn hard man to deal with. I can't help being ornery. I was born that way. And some men can't take it. Mulder is one of them, I guess. I reckon I rubbed him up the wrong way once too often, and when he flared up about it he couldn't settle down again. Bad blood built up between us.'

'You needled him badly on the night in question, refusing to take his IOU. He was so touchy about his honesty he even refused a loan from Wishart and insisted on getting some money from his own account.'

'Who have you been talking to? The way you say it, you could have been there.'

'That doesn't come into it. The fact is that if you hadn't persisted in baiting Mulder he wouldn't have dragged Wishart down into the bank, and the murder and robbery couldn't have taken place.'

'Are you saying that makes me responsible for what happened?' Whiteman started up off the sidewalk but groaned and slumped down again. 'Nobody could make Mulder do anything he didn't want to.'

'What do you think happened that evening? Is Mulder guilty?'

'I don't know.' Whiteman shook his head, and when he met Morgan's keen gaze he looked as if he was sorry for the way things had turned out. 'Looking at it, I fail to see how it could have been arranged. It happened in such a short time. I guess we were all shocked by the turn of events. Wishart dead, the money gone, and no sign of Mulder. If Mulder didn't do it then who did? Was there anyone in the bank waiting for them to go down? Or did they walk into something they weren't meant to?' Whiteman shook his head. 'That line of thinking is stretching coincidence too far. I'm baffled by what occurred, and the only way you'll get the answer is by talking to Mulder — if he's still alive and you can find him. He's sure covered his tracks if he did pull it off and made it away.'

Morgan realized that he would get nothing new from Whiteman and backed off, stepping back on to the sidewalk and looking around the street. Sheriff Cassidy was coming toward them at a fast walk, and Morgan turned away, not wanting to talk about what he had learned until he had assimilated the information.

'Is that it?' demanded Whiteman. 'Hell, you beat me up and give me all that aggravation, and then don't ask me anything worth knowing.'

'Is there anything you'd like to tell me?' Morgan countered. 'Got anything on your mind that I ought to know about?'

Whiteman shook his head. 'Like I said, if you want the truth of what happened that night you're gonna have to find Mulder.'

'If he's still alive I'll find him. You can bet on that. What's your interest in Jenny Mulder? I heard you say you reckoned it was time the business between you was settled.'

'I offered to buy Big G.' Whiteman got unsteadily to his feet and staggered as he tried to control his balance. 'The gal cain't run that place by herself. There's trouble on the range and it'll take a good man to get on top of it. Buying her out will do her a favour.'

'You expect her to sell up? She seems a mighty determined woman to me. She wouldn't give a second thought to selling, unless she was sure her father was dead. Then she might want to get out.'

Whiteman nodded. 'I got it doped out like that,' he admitted. 'But you can't blame a man for trying.'

'I suggest you don't bother her any more at this time.' A steel-like quality crept into Morgan's tone. 'I'm going to see her now, and I'll tell her you're dropping your interest in Big G as of this moment. She's got enough on her plate as it is. Do I make myself clear?'

Whiteman nodded. 'I ain't gonna argue with you, that's for sure.'

'I'll need to talk to you some more after I've had the opportunity of speaking to those others who were in the banker's apartment that evening.'

'You'll be able to find my spread if you need to come out there,' Whiteman conceded.

Morgan turned and walked into the hotel. He found Amos Henty behind the reception desk, and the excitement showing on the little clerk's face told Morgan that the man had witnessed the way Whiteman had been discomfited, and apparently approved of it. Henty's eyes were gleaming as he regarded Morgan.

'You sure taught Whiteman some manners,' he observed. 'I never thought I'd see the day when Hank Whiteman was forced to eat crow. I reckon they don't exaggerate your exploits, Mr Morgan.'

'Jenny Mulder is in the hotel,' Morgan said. 'What's her room number?'

'Twelve, on the top floor.'

Morgan ascended the stairs, and glanced back into the lobby to see if Henty was going to run to Draper to report. But the clerk remained behind the desk, pretending to be busy.

Jenny Mulder opened the door of the room almost as soon as Morgan had knocked, as if she had been standing inside waiting for him to call. He looked at her critically, trying to gauge her mood. Her face was composed, her lips set resolutely, but her pale eyes showed restlessness, and he could imagine the tortures she was suffering because of her missing father.

'I'm sorry to have to bother you at a time like this,' he said. 'You must be worried sick by what has happened.'

'Do you think my father is guilty?' she challenged, closing the door after he had entered. She motioned him to a seat by the window as he removed his hat, then sat down on the foot of the bed, gazing intently at him.

Morgan shook his head. 'I'm afraid I'm not in a position to judge. I'm still collecting the facts, and I ain't in the business of jumping to conclusions.'

'Make sure the facts you get from those present in the bank that night are true,' she said firmly. 'From what I've heard, most of them must be lying. My father was a strictly honest man through to his backbone. He drilled honesty into my brother and me from the time we were old enough to understand.'

'You have a brother? I haven't heard him mentioned. Where was he on the night of the murder?'

'In the cemetery, where he's been for the past five years.' Her tone flattened out as she spoke, and she blinked rapidly, as if trying to hold back tears. 'He was murdered. His killer was never found.'

Morgan frowned. 'What happened, and where?' he demanded.

'Dad found Johnny dead beside the

trail just out of town. Johnny had been returning home after a Saturday night out. His horse came on to the ranch riderless and Dad went to look for him. Johnny had been shot in the back, and the sheriff never found his killer.'

'So the history of this present trouble goes back at least five years,' Morgan mused. 'I reckoned it wasn't a simple case.'

'There's been trouble of one kind or another for as long as I can remember.' Jenny shook her head. 'We lost near three hundred head of cattle last year alone, and nobody knows who rustled them. I think my father would have done better to bring in a man like you to track down the rustlers, and perhaps his present trouble would have been avoided.'

'Did your father have any financial problems? Losing all those cattle last year must have strained his resources some, huh?'

'We managed, but only just. We had to take on more riders, and the wages bill is terrific. You have to pay through the nose for men who are willing to fight and die for a brand.'

Morgan nodded. 'You firmly believe that your father is innocent of the murder and robbery. Have you any facts to back you up?'

She shook her head slowly. 'There's nothing I can put my finger on. Dad didn't seem to be under more of a burden that Saturday, and I'm sure it would have shown in his manner if he had been planning a serious crime.'

Morgan got to his feet. 'Will you be staying long in town?'

'A few days. I had to get away from the ranch for a spell. It's driving me loco, not knowing one way or another what really happened that night.'

Morgan nodded sympathetically. 'I'll be seeing you again,' he promised, 'and if I get any news of your father you'll be the first to know about it.'

He took his leave, carrying with him a picture of her anguished face. His thoughts ran swiftly as he left the hotel and stood for a moment on the sidewalk. He had not learned much from Draper or Whiteman, Wishart was dead and Mulder missing, which left Ashby and Dan Meeker, the bank guard, to be questioned. He saw the sheriff standing in an alley-mouth, talking with Whiteman, and walked towards them. Whiteman saw his approach and departed swiftly for the saloon. Cassidy approached Morgan, shaking his head slowly.

'You've got a brand of law-dealing all of your own,' the sheriff remarked when they met. He lifted his Stetson and scratched his head.

'Was Whiteman complaining about the way I handled him?' Morgan looked towards the saloon and saw Whiteman standing by the batwings talking with the two men who had ridden into town with him. He wondered if the two were getting orders to get even for the HW rancher's discomfiture.

'Nope.' Cassidy grinned. 'In fact he seemed kinda pleased that you whaled the tar out of him. There ain't nobody else in this county could do that. What made you lay into him? Did he provoke you?'

'He didn't. It takes a great deal to provoke me. He was fairly spitting disrespect for the law so I decided to change his attitude. Now, Sheriff, I need to talk to Ashby and Mccker. And I'd like to look at the scene of the crime.'

'Mind if I tag along? I wanta see how a big Chicago detective works.'

'I never did handle a case in the big city.' Morgan grinned. 'I've worked everywhere else in my time, but usually on the range. I'd like to look at the bank now. I need to get a picture of the scene of the crime in my mind. Who's running the place?'

'James Wishart, Lew's son. He's worked in the bank ever since he was old enough to tot up a column of figures. What he doesn't know about banking ain't worth knowing. He's real cut up about his father's murder.'

'Where was he on the night in question?'

'Out at his ranch. He's got a small spread in Green Valley, about ten miles out of town. Him and his pa never saw eye to eye over his ranching activities. Lew wanted his son's whole attention on banking, but James always hankered on being a cattleman, and that caused friction between them. Mind you, Lew advanced James the cash to buy the spread. I guess blood is thicker than water, huh?'

They walked to the bank and Morgan looked around keenly when they entered. There was a counter with a grille just inside the door, and a railed-off area to the left, where the banker sat. A big safe stood in rear of the counter, and a door was to the left in the back wall. There was a teller behind the counter, and a man of about thirty-five years sat at the desk to the left. He was tall and well built, dressed in a good store suit. His fleshy face bore signs of grief in its set expression.

'That's James Wishart,' Cassidy said. 'Let's talk to him.'

The sheriff led the way to the desk and James Wishart got to his feet. He extended a hand when the sheriff made an introduction, and Morgan shook hands.

'I'm pleased to meet you,' Wishart said. 'The local investigation failed to discover what happened here that night, and I've been awaiting your arrival with great eagerness. We may now find out who murdered my father and robbed the bank.'

'You don't believe Gus Mulder did it?' Morgan asked.

'I'm hoping to marry Jenny Mulder,' James Wishart said. 'We've been courting a long time, so I got to know Gus pretty well. He was strictly honest. I can't bring myself to believe he's guilty, despite the evidence.'

'I hope to unravel this business pretty quick,' Morgan said. 'I'd like to look around, and also talk with Dan Meeker. I understand he was present that night.'

'Dan is off sick at the moment. He's

got a room at Ma Templeton's boarding-house.'

'Perhaps the sheriff can show me around and run through the events that took place according to the statements he gathered.'

'Certainly. I'll give you all the assistance I can. Good luck with your investigation. Call me if there's anything you need.' James Wishart returned to his desk.

'There's an outside flight of stairs in the alley to the left that leads up to the apartment overhead,' Cassidy explained. 'And there are stairs in the back room that give access from inside.' He led the way to the inner door and ushered Morgan into a big back room which was used as a store. A flight of stairs was to the left, and there was a rear door overlooking the back lots.

Morgan stood in the doorway and looked around the back room, then shifted his gaze to study the bank.

'So Wishart and Mulder came down the inner stairway and through this door into the bank. A few minutes later there were two shots, and when Meeker ran down those stairs shortly afterwards, what exactly did he find? Where was Wishart lying?'

'In front of the open safe.' Cassidy walked into the bank and moved to the safe. He tapped a spot with his booted toe. 'Right here is where he was lying. The safe door was open, the cash gone, and so was Mulder.'

'An outer door was left open,' Morgan mused. 'Which one? Front or back?'

'The back door.' Cassidy walked into the storeroom and approached the back door. It was locked and had two heavy bolts. Cassidy undid it and pulled it wide. He stepped aside for Morgan to inspect the scene, looking as if he expected the detective to come up with an immediate solution to the mystery.

Morgan checked the lock on the door, looking for marks that might suggest it had been tampered with. He found nothing. He stepped outside and looked around the back lots. There was a barn about twenty yards to the rear of the bank, and several cabins and shacks dotted around.

'Did you check who holds keys to the bank?' he asked.

'Sure did. Lew Wishart had keys to both doors. So does James Wishart. Dan Meeker has a key to the back door only. And the inner door between the storeroom and the bank is always kept locked when the bank is closed.'

Morgan nodded. 'Let's take a look upstairs now,' he suggested. 'The more I learn about this affair the more mystifying it looks.'

Cassidy led the way. The apartment above was large, with two bedrooms, a kitchen and a sitting-room. Morgan prowled around, trying to visualize what had happened on that fateful night. The sheriff watched him intently.

'How did Mulder get into town that day?' Morgan asked.

'Always rode a big grey.'

'Did he put it in the livery barn when he arrived?'

'Sure did. I got witnesses who saw him; talked to him before he went to the bank. The grey was still in the barn after the murder.'

'So Mulder walked away from the scene with twenty thousand dollars, didn't collect his horse from the stable, and no one saw him then or at any time afterwards.'

'That's about the weight of it.' Cassidy shook his head. 'Now you can see why I ain't had no luck with this case. I'm baffled, and I don't mind admitting it.'

'It is a poser. But I've still got two men to talk to. I'll take Meeker first. He's off work at the moment, huh? Any idea what's wrong with him?'

Cassidy shook his head. 'He was shocked by what happened that night. He dashed down the stairs before any of the others could recover from their shock, and found Wishart dead and blood all over the place.'

Morgan nodded. 'What about the second bullet that was fired?' he queried.

'I looked around after you mentioned it but couldn't find anything. Come and take a look for yourself and see if you can work out where the shots were fired from.'

They descended to the bank and Cassidy paused before the safe door.

'Wishart was lying here with his head towards the open safe and his feet pointing to the front door. There was a pool of blood here. I reckoned the killer shot him from close range. Probably standing right here.' The sheriff moved off a couple of paces and looked around. 'Two shots were fired, one hitting Wishart. I thought the second bullet might have gone into the open safe.'

'Unless it hit Mulder,' Morgan said softly. 'There are no two ways about this. If Mulder is guilty then he didn't stop a slug. And if he was shot then he wasn't responsible for the crime.

Wishart didn't have a gun and, being shot between the eyes, he wouldn't have had a chance of resisting if he had been armed.' He nodded. 'I'll talk to Meeker now. Thanks for your help, Sheriff. I'll check with you later.'

'Sure.' Cassidy spoke eagerly. 'Just let me know if there's anything I can help you with. I hope you do come up with the rights of it. I'm fair bursting to know what happened.'

Morgan left the bank and walked along the street, his mind seething with speculation as he tried to get to grips with what he had learned. He paused at the batwings of the saloon and peered inside to see Hank Whiteman bellied up to the bar with his two men. A man young enough to have been Whiteman's son, was in the company of the tough trio, swaying unsteadily, apparently tipsy. Morgan ran his eye over them. Whiteman reached out a large hand, grasped the youngster by his collar, and jerked him back to face the bar. Shaking his head, Morgan went on, and turned in at the doorway of Ma Templeton's guest house. A short, very fleshy lady emerged from a room to his left, enquiry showing on her ample face.

'I'm looking for Dan Meeker, ma'am.' Morgan removed his hat.

'He's not here at the moment. May I ask your business?'

'I'm a Pinkerton detective sent here to investigate the murder and bank robbery.'

'At last. Everyone in town has got tired of waiting for you to show up. I don't know what you expect to learn five weeks after the crime took place. But you're out of luck as far as Dan is concerned. He's taking a ride on the range. Doctor's orders. He had a bad shock when Lew Wishart was killed.'

'Any idea where Meeker went?'

'Said he was going out to James Wishart's ranch to do some work. He's nearly back to normal now, and reckons to return to work at the bank next week.'

'Thanks.' Morgan departed and went

along to the law office.

'Meeker can't help you?' The sheriff was seated at his desk.

Morgan explained the situation, and Cassidy grimaced.

'I never cottoned to that guy.' He spoke in a lowered tone. 'He don't look the type to do a hard day's work. Know what I mean? You can look at some men and tell exactly what they are, and I took a dislike to Meeker the first time I set eyes on him. I wouldn't mind betting there's a lot more to him than shows, and I ain't never far off the mark. Meeker comes across as a never-do-well. I remember being surprised when he got the job as shot-gun guard at the bank. It didn't seem right, somehow. But I must say that in the year he's been doing the job he hasn't put a foot wrong.'

'I'll get round to him when he returns from his outing.' Morgan consulted his notebook. 'I'm gonna see Sam Ashby now. Any idea where he might be at this time of the day?'

Cassidy consulted the clock on the wall. 'In his office in the saloon, I reckon. Sam's got his finger in many pies around here, and he sure works at his business. He owns the stable as well as the saloon, and he's currently the town mayor. But he's an all-right guy.'

'Thanks. Have you got a large-scale map of the county? I'd like to get my bearings in case I have to ride out.'

'Sure thing.' Cassidy pulled open a drawer and produced a map, which he spread out on the cluttered desk. He pointed out the boundaries of his bailiwick and then pinpointed the salient features. Morgan studied the locations of the various ranches until he was satisfied that he could ride to any of them without trouble.

'Thanks,' Morgan took his leave, and as he emerged from the office a gun was fired close by. A bullet smacked into the wall at his side.

5

As the heavy echoes of the shot rolled away across the town, Morgan lunged instinctively to his left and dived into the alley beside the law office. A bullet thudded into the wall beside his head and he felt the sting of a splinter that struck his left cheek. He ducked and drew his gun, then peered out of the alley, looking for the position of his attacker. He saw a puff of black gunsmoke drifting from an alley across the street. A movement showed over there, but the late-afternoon shadows were too dense for his gaze to pierce. He threw up his gun to fire, but the absence of a definite target made him change his mind. Instead, he ran across the street straight at the alley, staking his life on the thought that the ambusher would be running away.

Morgan reached the opposite side-walk without incident, and saw a figure leaving the other end of the alley, vanishing around a corner almost too quickly for his hard gaze to register details. All he got was a glimpse of a red shirt, and sunlight glinting on a silver hatband. He ran along the alley with loping strides, wondering at his attacker. Had his questions stirred some guilty person into taking this extreme course to avoid detection? Then his agile mind thrust up a picture of the tipsy youth who had been in the saloon with Hank Whiteman. He had been wearing a red shirt.

He paused at the far end of the alley and risked a quick glance around the corner. There was no movement any-where on the back lots and he breathed deeply to ease his tortured lungs.

His attacker had turned to the right out of the alley, and the only place along there that interested Morgan was the saloon. He ran in that direction, gun ready. Upon reaching the back door of the saloon, which opened to his touch, he bustled inside to find himself in a narrow passage. As he drew level with a door on the right it was jerked open and a man appeared in the opening.

'What's going on?' the newcomer demanded. 'It sounded like a herd of cattle.'

'Did someone just come in?' Morgan demanded.

'I heard feet on the board floor. They went by here into the public room. The back way is not for use by the public, you know. That's what the batwings are for. Who are you, and why are you holding a gun? I heard shots a few moments ago. Did you fire them? Has anyone been hurt?'

'Wait a minute.' Morgan went on and found an open doorway giving access to the bar. He entered and paused to look around the big room. The 'tender was turning away from the batwings. The place was otherwise deserted.

The 'tender paused when he saw

Morgan, then continued to the bar.

'You ain't supposed to come in the back way,' he observed.

'Someone came in ahead of me,' Morgan rapped. 'Who was it?'

'I ain't seen anyone. I heard shots outside and went for a looksee. Everyone piled out to see what was going on.'

'Where's Whiteman and his men now?' Morgan did not holster his gun.

'I told you. Everyone left when the shooting started.' The 'tender picked up a cloth and began polishing the bar.

Morgan spun around at the sound of feet behind him. He saw the man who had emerged from the room in the passage coming into the bar, and now he was carrying a double-barrelled shotgun.

'Are you Ashby?' Morgan demanded, ignoring the threat of the shotgun.

'That's right. Who in hell are you, coming in here like you owned the place?'

Morgan explained, and saw truculence die out of the man's expression.

Ashby was tall and lean, dressed in a smart blue store suit. He had an air of prosperity about him, and his manner proclaimed it. Aged about forty-five, his dark hair was thinning and receding, but his brown eyes looked ageless, narrowed and dull like a snake's. Displeasure lined the contours of his thin face. His hands were restless on the shotgun.

'I heard boots in the passage, Pete,' he said to the 'tender. 'Someone came in the back door fast. He passed my office and came in here. So where is he? There's no place else he could go.'

'I didn't see anyone,' the 'tender insisted. 'Like I said, I was outside on the sidewalk. There were two shots, and I was waiting for more. I didn't see anyone.'

'You're lying, mister.' Morgan's tone filled with sudden menace. 'If the man ain't in here then you let him out the batwings, and I want to know why you're keeping quiet about it. So tell me what is going on or you'll see the inside of the jail.'

The 'tender shook his head obstinately. At that moment the batwings were thrust open and the sheriff appeared, gun in hand. He paused to get his breath, then came towards Morgan, who was covering the 'tender with his gun.

Morgan explained what had happened, then said: 'Throw him in jail, Sheriff. I'll get around to him later. He's covering up for the man who shot at me, and I'll want some answers from him.' He studied the 'tender's face. 'Who was the young feller I saw with Whiteman when I looked in a few minutes ago? He was unsteady on his feet.'

The 'tender shook his head. 'I didn't see anyone like that with Whiteman. In any case, people in town keep clear of Whiteman and his crew.'

Morgan suppressed a sigh and waved an impatient hand. 'Slam the door on him, Sheriff,' he said. 'Maybe a spell behind bars will refresh his memory.'

Cassidy nodded and escorted the

'tender out of the saloon. Morgan turned to Ashby, who was regarding him steadily.

'I need to talk to you,' he said, 'and there's no time like the present so don't tell me you're too busy.'

'Wait till I get my manager down here,' Ashby replied. 'Would you like a drink? I might be a few minutes.'

'No thanks.' Morgan turned to the nearest table and dropped into a seat. He removed his hat and wiped sweat from his forehead, watching Ashby as the man ascended the stairs to the living-quarters above the saloon. He heard Ashby yelling for Billy Scarfe, and boots thudded overhead. A moment later Ashby descended the stairs, followed closely by the manager.

'This is the limit,' Scarfe complained as he went behind the bar. 'Where am I gonna get another 'tender from at this time of the day? It'll get real busy in here later. I'll be rushed off my feet.'

'Mattie will come in,' Ashby said. 'She always helps out.'

'You know I don't like my gal in here,' Scarfe responded.

Ashby joined Morgan at the table and sat down opposite. Morgan questioned him at length about Lew Wishart's murder and the bank robbery, and was not surprised when he learned nothing new from the saloon-man. Ashby answered him willingly enough, but said nothing beyond the bare facts. Changing the subject abruptly, Morgan asked:

'What do you know about Cass Frayne?'

'Frayne?' Ashby's eyes narrowed but his face did not change expression. He thought for a few moments, then shook his head slowly. 'Who is he?' he asked. 'I've never heard of him.'

'He's dead now — stabbed a short time ago in the stable.'

Ashby's face paled despite his admirable control. 'What's going on around here?' he demanded. 'There's nothing but trouble these days.'

'By all accounts, the trouble started a

long time ago. It's only now coming to a head. You must know Frayne. He's the gunslinger you brought into town. He stayed under cover in a room in your house until after Lew Wishart was killed. Then he disappeared from the scene until he staggered out of the stable today with a knife in his chest.'

'I don't know where you got that information from but it's all wrong.' Ashby laughed in a brittle tone. 'What would I want with a gunslinger, for God's sake? I never ever heard of Frayne, and certainly didn't see anyone like him around here. You must have got me mixed up with someone else. Who have you been talking to?'

'That don't make no never mind. I got witnesses who will swear it's the truth, so you better come clean and tell me what was going on. I guess Frayne's business was to do with the bank robbery, huh? That's the only conclusion I can reach. So start telling me exactly what happened that night.'

'I swear to God I don't know

anything about it.' Ashby leaned forward and gazed earnestly into Morgan's impassive face. 'There are others around town you should be talking to instead of me.'

'That's a fact.' Morgan agreed. 'So just name them and I'll take your advice. Apart from learning why Frayne was around town secretly, I need to know why he was killed today, and by whom. Someone stuck a knife in Frayne to shut his mouth. A real live killer is walking around here, probably with the knowledge of who committed some of the crimes that have taken place lately. And, Ashby, your best course is to come clean about your part in it. I'm not gonna give up, you know. Now I've got my teeth into the case I'll worry it until my answers drop out. So do us all a favour and speak up.'

'I don't believe this,' Ashby said hollowly. 'I'm the town mayor, among other things. I stand for law and order. I've been trying to light a fire under the sheriff to get something done about the lawlessness we're suffering. No one else in town has the slightest interest in improving our standard of life. I was the one who insisted we get in expert help; they send for you, and it looks like I'm your main suspect.'

'Finish your protests so we can get down to the real business.' A hard note sounded in Morgan's quiet voice. 'How many present in Wishart's apartment that night were in on the robbery? I'll accept that the murder wasn't a part of the deal but happened when Wishart resisted. That's why things went wrong. Or was it Mulder who didn't go along with it? He was strictly honest, I've heard.'

'You must be loco if you think along those lines.' Ashby stood up from the table, almost overturning his chair as he did so, and Morgan reached out a long arm, seized him by the front of his shirt, and dumped him back in the seat.

'I'll tell you when I've finished asking questions,' he rapped. 'This is a murder enquiry, and you're in the hot seat right now. Listen to how I think things shaped up that night. I have the basic facts, and this is what I make of them. The bank doors weren't forced or broken open so someone used keys. How or where they got them from I'll go into later. So there was more than one man in on the steal. The bank robbery was timed to happen during the evening because Wishart would be engaged in playing poker. But White-man needled Mulder just a bit too much, and when Mulder insisted on drawing money from his account, Wishart decided to humour him. They went down into the bank and walked straight into the robbery, with the result that Wishart died and Mulder disap-peared.'

Ashby shook his head as he listened. 'I don't accept a word of that,' he said. 'It's utter nonsense. There was no one in the bank that evening when Wishart and Mulder went down.'

'I think there was,' Morgan insisted. 'But what mystifies me is why Mulder wasn't shot in cold blood and left as Wishart was. Perhaps Mulder was in with the gang. That is the only logical answer.'

'Are there any more questions you want to ask me?' Ashby almost stuttered in his agitation and ran a finger around the inside of his collar. His face was ashen, his eyes showing stress. 'Look, I'm a busy man, and I don't need to waste my time listening to your hot air.'

'It'll be all for the moment.' Morgan smiled as pure relief crossed Ashby's face. 'I'll be coming back to you later though, so don't leave town. You better think deeply about what I've said. The next time we talk I shall want satisfying answers from you. I'm gonna clean up around here. That's what I was hired for, and that's what I'm gonna do.'

Ashby sprang up from his seat as if it were hot and hurried out of the bar. Morgan heard the door of the man's office slam a moment later, and leaned back in his seat to consider what he had learned. Ashby had not answered one of his questions directly, but had given some useful information indirectly.

Morgan got up and crossed to the bar. Scarfe appeared to be busy polishing the woodwork, and did not look up when Morgan confronted him.

'Beer,' Morgan said. He waited until a foaming glass was slid before him, and slapped a coin on the bar top. 'You been working here long?' he queried.

'About seven years.' Scarfe looked at him but his gaze was unsteady, sliding away before Morgan could look directly into his eyes. 'Why do you ask?'

'Seven years, huh? So you should know everybody in town.'

'I reckon so.'

Morgan described the youthful man who had been at the bar with Whiteman. 'You know who I'm talking about?' he asked. 'He looked like he was a regular customer. He was unsteady, as if he had been drinking all day.'

'Could be any of a number of men.

What was he wearing, did you say?'

'A red shirt.' Morgan recalled the glimpse he had got of the man he had followed along the alley. 'He looked like a dude cowboy, someone who gets a kick out of dressing the part but can't even sit a horse.'

'Red shirt, huh? What about his hat? Was it black, and decorated with a band of silver conchos?' Scarfe poured himself a whiskey and glanced furtively towards the back door before gulping it.

'You got it.' Morgan nodded eagerly. 'That was his hat. Does the description fit anyone you know?'

'Yep. You're talking about Al Raynor. He's the only one I know who dresses like a dude, and he sure ain't done a day's work in the time I've known him. He's nothing but a troublemaker. Nearly always tipsy, and always on the prod. If you look twice at him when he's in one of his moods he'll like as not put a slug in your brisket.'

Morgan nodded. 'What kind of a horse does he ride?'

'Big buckskin stallion. When did you see Raynor?'

'He was in here about fifteen minutes ago, in the company of Hank Whiteman. Did you hear the two shots that were fired?'

'Yeah, but I don't take any notice of that kind of thing these days. There's always someone ready to trigger a gun. You should have heard the HW outfit when they left town earlier. It must cost them a hatful of dollars for cartridges.'

'Any idea how Raynor occupies himself when he's in town?'

'He lives in town. Never leaves it, far as I know. If he ain't drinking, which he does more than eating, then he'll be chasing after some woman. I had to lay down the law to him when he took an interest in my gal Mattie. I want her to do well for herself, but she couldn't do worse than Al Raynor.'

'Has he got a rich father?'

'Not that I know of.' Scarfe shook his head. 'What makes you ask that?'

'He's got no visible means of

support, yet he dresses well and is never short of a dollar.'

'I don't know a damn thing about his business, and wouldn't question it even if I was interested.' Scarfe helped himself to another whiskey. 'It ain't safe to ask questions.'

'Sure.' Morgan nodded. 'Thanks for the information. See you around.' He emptied his glass and departed.

He paused on the sidewalk and looked around. His lips compressed when he saw Hank Whiteman and his two men emerging from the stable, leading their horses. They mounted and came along the street at a steady trot. Morgan expected them to draw weapons and start hoorahing the town, but they passed him quietly, and did not even look in his direction. He watched them out of sight before he moved, and then strode along the sidewalk to the law office.

Cassidy was seated at his desk when Morgan walked in on him. The sheriff looked up, smiling a greeting, but his face was set in serious lines, his eyes showing concern.

'You lost some money, Sheriff?' Morgan demanded.

'Money?' Cassidy shook his head. 'What do you mean?'

'You look like you lost a silver dollar and found a wooden nickel.'

Cassidy frowned. 'I'm concerned about the way you're handling your investigation,' he said slowly.

'You can speak your mind freely.' Morgan sat down on a corner of the desk. 'But before you do, just tell me one thing. How much have you learned about the bank robbery since it happened five weeks ago?'

'Next to nothing.'

'Nothing in a whole month or more.' Morgan nodded. 'I ain't been in town more than two hours and I got the reins of my investigation well and truly in hand. I'm pulling the pieces together, and with any luck we'll have the whole story laid bare before the end of the week. So don't feel concerned about my manner of handling the investigation. It is intended to get results, which is happening. By the way, that man who was stabbed down at the stable. Have you got anything on him yet, or the knife that was stuck in him?'

Cassidy shook his head. 'I've asked around, and some of the men in town have viewed the body. He's a stranger. As for the knife, there's nothing special about it.'

'His name is Cass Frayne. He was a gunslinger. I have a feeling he was brought in to handle the bank robbery.'

'What?' Cassidy gazed at Morgan, his mouth agape in disbelief. 'How in hell did you learn that much about him?'

'I can't explain my methods. But he looks like a stranger because he didn't show himself around town during the time he was here. He came before the bank robbery, and disappeared after it happened. I don't know where he's been during the last five weeks, but he showed up today to die at the stable.'

'Where was he hiding in town before

the robbery?' Cassidy demanded. 'I can't believe that. If he was around then someone would have seen him.' He paused for a moment, looking thoughtful, then asked: 'Who brought him in to rob the bank?'

'That's something I can't tell you at the moment. There's a youngster by the name of Al Raynor lives in town. What can you tell me about him?'

'He's no good. I wish I could put him going but he's always got plenty of dough so I can't hit him for vagrancy. I reckon he's mixed up in some of the crime we're getting, but I can't pin anything on him. What have you got on him?'

'Did you hear two shots a short while ago?'

'Yeah. But I don't take any notice of that kind of thing these days.' Cassidy spoke in a long-suffering tone. 'If I did I'd never get to sit down at this desk. It's getting so a man can't find a peaceful spot anywhere in town. There's always something going on, and none of it good.'

'I'm certain Raynor fired those shots at me.' Morgan explained what had occurred. 'Thanks for bringing in that 'tender. I'll be talking to him again later. Have you got any idea where I'd find Raynor now? He was with Hank Whiteman in the saloon when I passed on my way here earlier, and he was waiting in the alley across the street when I left.'

'Do you think Whiteman put him up to shooting at you?' Cassidy looked troubled. 'I don't know who's causing the trouble around here, but I know where the guilt is pointed. To my way of thinking it's got to be Whiteman. And lately, his son Buck has started acting up, mixing with undesirables, drinking and gambling, making a general nuisance of himself. Of course, Buck is running around with Al Raynor. They are two of a kind.'

'So where does Raynor hit the sack when he's not living it up in town?'

'In a cabin off the main street, almost behind the general store. He shares it with a couple of other nogoods — Danny Wymer and Roy Benton.'

'Do they work regularly at anything?'

'Anything is about right. They don't hold down regular jobs. Do you wanta go along and meet those guys?'

'I'd sure like to talk to Raynor right now.'

Cassidy slid off his seat, hitched up his sagging gunbelt, and stalked to the door. They left the office, and Morgan sided the sheriff along the street. Cassidy passed the front of the store and turned into an alley. Morgan was acutely aware of his surroundings, his keen gaze flitting around, and he kept his right hand close to the butt of his holstered gun. When they reached the back lots, Cassidy paused and pointed to a ramshackle wooden building standing some twenty yards back from the alley.

'That's where Raynor and the others live. They rent the place off Sam Ashby, who owns the store.'

'Ashby is a man of property, isn't he?'

'Yep. He owns the saloon and the livery barn, and he's got a ranch out by Alder Creek called the S Bar A. The creek is the place Mulder and Whiteman had their differences over. Shall we go and see if Raynor and his pards are at home? My guess is that they'll be sleeping off the effects of last night's carousing. I never see Benton or Wymer around town during the day. But I see them at all times during the night, when I'm making my rounds. They're night birds right enough.'

'Let's pay them a visit.' Morgan eased his gun. He flexed the fingers of his right hand. 'Someone around town knows all there is to know about Wishart's death and the bank robbery and, from what I've learned, this trio look favourite for the honour.'

'Why don't you let me talk to them in the first place?' Cassidy suggested. 'You're a stranger, and if they're guilty they might panic at the sight of you.'

'Only if they've got a guilty conscience,' Morgan opined. 'Let's go flush them out, Sheriff. This might be the break you've been praying for.'

They crossed the back lots and paused before the heavy door of the cabin. Cassidy hurried over the last few strides to draw ahead of Morgan, and knocked on the door with a heavy fist.

'Hello, inside,' he called. 'This is Sheriff Cassidy. I need to talk to you fellers.'

Morgan did not relax, and there was a frown on his angular face as he waited. He would have preferred to handle this business differently, and when several shots hammered inside the cabin, he knew he should have taken better precautions. Bullets crackled through the door from inside and, instinctively ducking out of the line of fire, he saw Cassidy spin around and fall heavily.

6

With the raucous crash of shooting ringing in his ears, Morgan dived behind the left-hand corner of the building. He glanced over his shoulder at the sheriff's inert body, his lips tightening when he saw blood on Cassidy's shirt. His gun was in his hand but he did not recall drawing it. Harsh echoes were hammering inside his head as he moved swiftly along the side of the cabin, passed along the rear wall, and eased to the front corner on the opposite side of the building. Reaching the corner, he peered around it to see that the sheriff was still motionless where he had fallen, and at that moment the door of the cabin creaked open and two men came out fast, guns in their hands. They split up, running in opposite directions, making for two different alleys leading to the street.

Morgan yelled for them to stop. The nearer man half-turned, his gun swinging, and fired a shot in Morgan's direction. The bullet clipped the corner of the cabin before Morgan raised his gun. Aiming deliberately, he shot the man in the left thigh, and turned his gun on the second man, who had turned at bay, his gun swinging quickly. Morgan fired again, this time aiming for the right shoulder. The man tumbled to the hard ground. Morgan watched him for a moment then went to the half-open door of the cabin and kicked it wide. He looked inside, the muzzle of his gun steady.

The cabin was deserted. He turned to the sheriff, dropping to one knee beside the lawman's inert figure. Cassidy had been hit in the upper chest. He was unconscious. Morgan examined him and found the wound bleeding slightly. Morgan went across to the first of the two men, who was conscious and gripping his left thigh. Blood was showing through his fingers.

The man reached for his gun as Morgan approached him, and Morgan fired a shot that struck the weapon and sent it skittering out of reach. He stood over the man, who looked up with glowering desperation in his fleshy face.

'What's your name?' Morgan demanded.

The man shook his head, his teeth clenched against increasing pain.

'Get rid of any more weapons you might have,' Morgan said tersely. 'And be quick about it.'

'I ain't armed now,' the man muttered.

Morgan holstered his gun and dropped to one knee, searching the man with practised ease. He pulled a small hideout gun from inside the man's jacket and dropped it into his own pocket, then found an empty sheath on the right side of the man's belt.

'Where's your knife?' he asked.

'I lost it a coupla days ago. Get the doctor, will you? I'm like to bleed to death.'

Morgan arose and approached the

second man, who was unconscious. He checked the motionless figure for weapons and, as he straightened, caught a glimpse of movement in the mouth of the nearest alley. He looked around and saw Mike Bradley, the deputy sheriff, stepping into view, a gun in his hand.

'Fetch the doctor,' Morgan called. 'Cassidy has been shot and looks pretty bad.'

Bradley nodded and turned away instantly. Morgan could hear the sound of his feet receding back along the alley. He bent and took hold of the unconscious man's collar and dragged him to the side of the other man.

'Why did you start shooting when the sheriff called out to you?' Morgan asked.

'It wasn't me,' the man replied. 'It was Wymer, the damn hothead! He was asleep on his bunk and the sheriff's voice startled him awake. He sprang up and grabbed his gun. Before I knew what was happening, he started shooting through the door.'

'So he's got a guilty conscience, huh?' Morgan nodded. 'Why did you start running when he came out of the shack? And when I shouted for you to halt you threw a slug at me.'

'I wasn't trying to hit you. For God's sake, where's that doctor?'

'If he's Wymer then you must be Benton,' Morgan suggested.

The man cursed him in a pain-filled tone.

Morgan went back to where the sheriff was lying. Cassidy had come back to his senses, and smiled uncertainly as Morgan dropped to one knee beside him. The sheriff's face was gaunt, pale with shock, and his eyes showed pain.

'I guess I made a mistake, huh?' he muttered.

'You'll be all right,' Morgan told him. 'The doctor will be here soon. Just take it easy.'

'Who was in the shack? Why did they start shooting?'

Morgan explained and the sheriff

nodded and closed his eyes.

'Watch out for Al Raynor now,' he mumbled, and lapsed into unconsciousness.

Morgan heard footsteps approaching and looked up to see Bradley returning, pushing through a gathering crowd of curious onlookers, with Bill Caylin following with a leather bag. When the doctor paused beside Wymer, Morgan called to him.

'Over here first, Doc. Those two can wait. The sheriff is more seriously hurt.'

Caylin hurried across and dropped to one knee beside the sheriff. He checked the lawman's condition, then reached into his medical bag for a bandage. Looking up at Bradley, he said:

'Mike, take the door off the cabin and get some of those men to help you. Get Cassidy to my place as fast as you can, but go gently. Tell my wife to ready him for an operation. I'll be along as soon as I can.'

The deputy nodded and signalled to the watching men. Several came forward as Morgan went to where he had left Wymer and Benton. He scanned the faces of the dozen or so men forming a circle around them, looking for the man he had seen with Whiteman in the saloon.

'Has anyone seen Al Raynor in the last half-hour?' he asked generally.

'I saw him about twenty minutes ago,' a man volunteered. 'He was going into Helen's dress shop along the street, and looked like he was in a big hurry.'

'Mebbe he was gonna buy a new dress,' someone observed, and there was raucous laughter from the crowd.

Morgan stood watchful and alert until the doctor approached. Bradley passed, following the four men carrying Cassidy on the cabin door.

'Come to the office when you've finished with the sheriff,' Morgan called to the deputy, and Bradley nodded.

The doctor busied himself with the two wounded men and, when they were fit to be moved, Morgan had them carried along to the jail. Bradley returned as the prisoners were being removed, and Morgan asked him to take control at the jail.

'Put Wymer and Benton in the cells and don't let anyone in to see or speak to them,' he said. 'And don't let them speak to each other.'

'What are you gonna do?' Bradley asked.

'I need to check the cabin for clues, and then I'm gonna pick up Al Raynor,' Morgan replied.

Bradley moved off after the crowd escorting the two prisoners to the jail and Morgan went to the cabin. He paused in the open doorway, studying the interior before entering. It was untidy, cluttered with discarded clothing, used plates and cooking utensils. There was a scarcity of furniture — three single bunks, a table, three chairs, and little else. Morgan stepped inside and began a thorough search, starting just inside the doorway and working his way across the single room.

When he found nothing of interest, he stood in the centre of the room and looked around before moving on to the second stage of the search. Then he began to check all the more obvious places where a man might hide something he wished to keep secret. He searched the floor space inch by inch, looking for spots where the well-trodden earth had been disturbed recently, and found nothing. Moving on to the fireplace, he checked each individual stone, looking for any that were loose, for a cavity beneath a stone in the hearth was a popular hiding-place with cabin dwellers.

A big flat stone moved fractionally when he pushed his hand against it, and Morgan paused for a moment, then took hold of the stone and exerted his strength. The stone moved with a grating sound, then came up out of the hearth. Morgan put it quickly to one side, reached into the cavity and took hold of a package that was wrapped in a waterproofed cloth.

Moving to the table, Morgan sat down and unwrapped the cloth, his eyes glinting when he revealed a wad of paper money that was held together by a wide paper band bearing a printed legend: CATTLEMAN'S BANK — TURKEY CREEK. He counted the money. There were $3,000 in the wad.

Footsteps sounded outside the door and Morgan palmed his .44 as a shadow darkened the doorway. The muzzle of his Smith & Wesson lined up on the chest of the newcomer as he stepped into the cabin. It was the man Morgan had seen in Hank Whiteman's company in the saloon earlier, wearing the red shirt he had spotted on his ambusher in the alley.

'Say, where in hell has the door gone?' Al Raynor demanded, squinting at Morgan's dim figure at the table. 'Hey, you ain't Danny or Roy . . . ' His voice trailed off when he saw the gun in Morgan's hand. 'You got the advantage of me, mister,' he finally acknowledged.

'Glad to see you.' Morgan got to his feet, his gun steady, the muzzle an unwinking black eye that posed a threat of death to the newcomer. 'I was about to come looking for you so you've saved me considerable trouble. I assume you're Al Raynor, and I want to talk to you about a couple of shots that were fired at me earlier from the alley opposite the law office. But that can wait. It's more important to me to learn how this money came to be hidden here under the hearth. Is it yours?'

'Money? Heck, I never have more than two cents to rub together.' Raynor stood with his hands held out from his sides. 'Where are my two pards? You're that Pinkerton man everyone is talking about, ain't you? I heard you'd showed up.'

'Where have you been?' Morgan demanded. 'Didn't you hear the shooting that took place here about half an hour ago? Sheriff Cassidy was shot down without warning by either Wymer or Benton, and when they ran for it I downed them. Benton took a slug in the leg and Wymer caught one in the chest. They're both in jail now, just waiting for you to join them.'

'Why should you think I'm involved in anything those two have been up to?' Raynor grinned. 'Just because we live together to save expenses.'

'We'll go into that more fully in the law office.' Morgan approached the man to snake his holstered gun out of leather and, as his fingers closed around the butt, Raynor swung to grapple with him. But Morgan had been expecting such a move and crashed the barrel of his .44 against Raynor's left temple. 'That was a foolish thing to do,' he observed as Raynor sprawled on the floor. 'You were saying you're innocent, but your actions indicate otherwise. On your feet. We got some talking to do.'

He checked Raynor's gun before thrusting it into his waistband, finding two empty cartridges in the cylinder. Sniffing the muzzle, he decided that the weapon had been fired quite recently. He scooped up the paper money and thrust it into a jacket pocket as Raynor got unsteadily to his feet.

'You know where the jail is,' Morgan said, motioning with his gun, 'so get moving. I reckon you can tell me a great deal about the case I'm working on.'

Raynor walked submissively enough to the jail, although he cast several glances over his shoulder at Morgan, who stayed out of reach. Mike Bradley, seated behind the desk, looked up when Raynor entered the office with Morgan a couple of paces behind. The deputy got to his feet and grinned as he pulled up a chair for Raynor.

'Before we start,' Morgan said briskly, for the record, 'Mike, can you identify this prisoner?'

'Sure, he's Al Raynor,' the deputy replied.

'Good. That's all I want to know. Turn out your pockets, Raynor, before you sit down.' Both lawmen watched Raynor until he had complied, and then Morgan searched him. 'Now unbuckle your gunbelt,' Morgan continued. He produced the wad of notes he had

143

found in the cabin and tossed it on the desk, watching the deputy's face for expression. Bradley's eyes widened when he saw the paper band and read the words printed on it.

'Hey, this must be part of the money stolen from the bank when Wishart was killed,' he exclaimed. 'Where did you find it?'

Morgan explained, and stood over Raynor. 'If you know what's good for you, then start talking,' he advised. 'Murder was committed the night the bank was robbed, and somebody is gonna hang for that. Were you involved in the robbery and subsequent events?'

'Was I hell! Don't try to pin that on me.'

'No one is going to pin anything on anyone,' Morgan said quietly. 'If you were not involved then go ahead and prove it. Where were you on the night in question?'

'I was out of town, visiting a woman, if you must know.'

Morgan nodded. 'Fine. What's her

name? I'll check with her. Did you know the robbery was to take place? Is that why you left town — to set up an alibi?'

'I heard some talk, that's all, and knowing the kind of reputation I got around here I didn't want to take any chances of being accused.'

'So who is the woman you saw that night?'

Raynor shook his head. 'I won't reveal her name. It would cause too much trouble.'

'Your neck is in a noose at the moment,' Morgan pointed out. 'So what do you call too much trouble? You needn't be afraid that the woman's name will come out as a result of my investigation. It will not pass beyond these walls. So start talking, Raynor, or you'll find out what trouble really is. All I want to do is pin the guilt where it belongs. If you're not involved then you've got nothing to worry about. We've got the deadwood on your two pards, Benton and Wyner. One of them shot the sheriff — Wymer, if Benton is to be believed. But we can easily get to the truth of that matter. Then they've got to explain how three thousand dollars of stolen money came to be concealed under the hearth in the cabin.'

'I didn't know about the money,' Raynor said, scowling. 'They called themselves my pards, and kept quiet about all that dough!' He shook his head. 'I'm in the dark as much as anyone else when it comes to that robbery. I don't know what happened, or if Gus Mulder is alive or dead. That's the gospel truth. You've got to believe me.'

'Sure.' Morgan smiled. 'I'll accept your story until I get evidence to the contrary. We'll let it ride until after I've questioned Benton and Wymer. Now let's get back to who took a couple of shots at me about an hour ago. On my way to this office to talk to the sheriff, I happened to see you in the saloon talking with Hank Whiteman. When I left the office I was fired upon. Two shots that just missed me came out of the alley opposite. I gave chase, and spotted my attacker leaving the far end of the alley. He was dressed in a red shirt just like you, and looked to be about your build.'

'It wasn't me. Heck, I ain't got the only red shirt in town.'

'I checked your gun when I took it off you. There are two empty cartridges in the cylinder, and the barrel smells as if it was fired recently.' Morgan took the pistol from his belt. 'Is this your gun?' he demanded, and Raynor nodded. Morgan handed the weapon to Bradley. 'Check it,' he said.

There was silence while the deputy examined the pistol.

'Yep,' he said at length. 'Just like you said. Two empty cartridges, and it has been fired within the last hour.'

'I fired a couple of shots at a rat back of the general store,' Raynor countered.

'Lock him up,' Morgan said. 'Can you put him so there's no contact between him, Wymer and Benton?'

'Sure.' Bradley nodded. 'We got some special cells for cases like this. What are you gonna charge him with?'

'Shooting at me. I spotted him right enough. It'll do to hold him on. We'll get a statement from him later. Right now we better talk to Benton and Wymer.'

'They're both in cells,' Bradley said. 'Benton is conscious and can be questioned, but Wymer was unconscious when I checked him just before you came in. The doctor gave him something to make him sleep.'

Raynor was escorted into the cell block and placed in a single cell to the left of the door. He turned and looked at Morgan as the door was locked.

'I wanta see the lawyer, Jonas Draper,' he said. 'He'll soon get me outa here.'

'Don't count on it,' Morgan advised him. He locked the door, cutting off Raynor's protests, and grasped Bradley's arm. 'Before we talk to Benton, where's the knife that was sticking in Cass Frayne's chest?'

'In the safe in the office. It's got a label on it with details of where and how it was found.'

'Fetch it, and remove the label. Benton is wearing an empty sheath on his belt, and when I asked him what happened to his knife he said he lost it a couple of days ago.'

'Do you think he killed Frayne with it?' Excitement echoed in Bradley's voice.

'That's what I aim to find out. Where is Benton?'

'Four doors along on the other side of the entrance.' Bradley went into the office and Morgan walked to the door of Benton's cell.

Benton was lying on the bunk in the cell, staring up at the ceiling. The left leg of his pants had been cut open and a bandage showed where the doctor had treated him. Morgan waited until Bradley came back with the knife, then took the weapon and held it down at his side as they entered the cell. Benton looked at them, and then closed his eyes.

'I got nothing to say to you,' he rasped.

'I got plenty to say to you,' Morgan responded. 'Take a look at this. I found your knife for you.'

Benton's eyes opened swiftly and he gazed at the knife in Morgan's hand.

'No,' he said with a grin. 'That ain't mine. I told you I lost mine a couple of days ago. I was on a trip to Clayton Junction, so you couldn't find it around here. That one you've got doesn't even look like mine.'

Morgan held out his hand for the cell keys and Bradley passed them over without comment. Morgan went back to Raynor's cell and unlocked the door. He held out the knife in his left hand, keeping his right hand close to the butt of his holstered gun.

'Benton tells me this is your knife,' he said, holding out the blade for Raynor's inspection.

'What in hell is he trying to pull?' Raynor scowled. 'I never carry a knife, and that one belongs to Benton.'

'Are you sure about that?'

'Of course I'm sure. I've seen Benton enough times with it. He's always throwing it at a target. The inside of the cabin door is peppered by it. Say, where did the cabin door go?'

'Will you testify in court that this is Benton's knife?' Morgan persisted.

'I will if Benton is saying it belongs to me. Ask Wymer if you don't believe me.'

Morgan nodded and departed. He went back to Benton's cell and confronted the prisoner. Bradley was standing in the open doorway, his hand on the butt of his gun, gazing stolidly at the man on the bunk.

'This knife has been identified as yours,' Morgan said. 'I've got a witness who will stand up in court and testify to that fact.'

'I already told you I lost my knife a couple of days ago.'

'You're keen on making a point of when you lost it. I'll tell you where I saw it earlier this afternoon. It was sticking in the chest of Cass Frayne, a gunman suspected of being involved in the bank robbery five weeks ago.'

'Never heard of Frayne.' Benton shook his head.

'You're connected with that bank robbery,' Morgan insisted. 'I found three thousand dollars in your cabin so don't try to convince me you know nothing about it.'

Benton gazed at Morgan without speaking, a bleak expression on his sharp features.

'Well?' Morgan demanded sharply. 'How do you answer that charge?'

'I don't know anything about it,' Benton said doggedly, and Morgan knew by the tone in his voice that nothing more could be learned from him at this time.

'So, as far as you're concerned, the guilt lies with either Raynor or Wymer, or both of them.'

'I didn't say that.'

'That is what you're implying.' Morgan's tone was severe. 'If you don't want me jumping to conclusions then you'd better say something in your defence.'

'I want to see Draper, the lawyer. He'll get me out of this.'

'It looks like Draper is going to be busy around here for the next few days,' Morgan observed. 'All right, I'll let him know that you and Raynor want to see him. But you'd better think carefully about your position. I'll be back to ask more questions later.'

Morgan backed out of the cell and Bradley joined him. The deputy locked the cell door, and he was grinning when he looked at Morgan, who peered into Wymer's cell to see the man still apparently unconscious on his bunk.

'You got him and Raynor worried. I admire you, Morgan. Following the murder and robbery, the sheriff ran around town like a chicken with its head cut off, and never learned a thing

153

about the case. You ain't been in town only two shakes and you've nearly solved it.'

Morgan shook his head. 'There's a long way to go yet,' he declared. 'I've got a picture forming in my head from what I heard from the various witnesses, and there are one or two significant pointers we can use as levers against those who are leaning towards guilt. But I need to talk to Dan Meeker before I start pulling the strings tight. The sheriff told me he didn't cotton to Meeker nohow. How do you see him?'

'Cassidy has had much more experience in handling the law than me,' Bradley said doubtfully. 'I'm a johnny-come-lately. I don't like Meeker, but that don't make him bad. Yet there is something about him that leaves a bad taste in the mouth. I can't put my finger on it exactly.'

'I'll be looking him up soon as I can,' Morgan said. 'I heard that he's out of town today.'

'I saw him on Main Street when I

was going for the doc,' Bradley said. 'Wherever he's been, he's back now.'

'I'll go look him up then. Any idea where I'll find him?'

'He'll be in the saloon, if I know him.'

'Have you got any help to run this place while the sheriff is on his back?'

'Yeah. Don't worry. There are a couple of men I can call on who are ready to back the law if needed.'

'See you later then. I'll be back soon. I want to question Raynor and Benton some more, and talk to those two men the sheriff jailed for me. They stuck me up when I emerged from the saloon. I figure Draper set me up for that, but he denied it when I questioned him.' Morgan shook his head. 'At the moment it seems that everyone in town is involved in this.'

'Watch your back around town,' Bradley warned. 'There's a killer hiding out somewhere. Wishart was killed, and then there was Frayne. This trouble ain't over, not by a long rope.'

Morgan nodded and went out to the street. He was surprised to see the evening was well advanced. Shadows were creeping into the corners and alleys, and he checked his surroundings with a keen eye before moving along the sidewalk. He went to the saloon and peered in over the batwings. There were at least a dozen men inside, and he wondered which of them was Dan Meeker. He pushed open the swing doors, then paused in the act of entering for his gaze fell upon a big man standing at the bar talking to Billy Scarfe, who was wiping glasses.

Morgan stepped back outside again, eased to an adjacent window and peered through, narrowing his gaze as he studied the man at the bar. The big figure had looked familiar, and Morgan was casting back through his mind for a name to go with it. He noted that Scarfe had glanced towards the door as he changed his mind about entering, then leaned forward and said something quietly to the man, who threw a glance towards the batwings.

When he saw the man full-face, Morgan palmed his gun and cocked it as he thrust through the batwings, his memory instantly producing a name to go with the face. Jake Billing, a hold-up man and cold-blooded killer, who had eluded Morgan in a big case some five years before.

7

Morgan held his gun jammed against his right hip as he strode to the bar, studying the killer, ensuring that he was indeed the man he suspected. Billy Scarfe glanced at him, then spoke warningly to Jake Billing, who glanced casually towards the batwings. Billing recognized Morgan immediately, for he spun away from the bar and reached for his gun in a fast draw. Morgan fired a shot that struck Billing's pistol in its holster before the killer could touch it. The hammering crash bludgeoned the silence, freezing everyone in the saloon except two men over to the left, seated at a small gaming-table. Morgan glimpsed their movement from a corner of his eye as they leapt to their feet and pulled their guns.

Morgan stepped in close to Billing, his pistol rising and falling as he crashed the barrel against the outlaw's head. He grabbed Billing before the man could fall to the sanded floor. Stepping in behind Billing, Morgan swung to face the new threat, covering himself with the slumping figure he was holding upright. Guns blasted and slugs crashed into the back-bar mirror, almost fanning Morgan's head in passing. He saw the two men over by the far wall with their smoking guns pointing in his direction. They were upturning their table for cover.

Morgan lifted his gun around the inert Billing and triggered the weapon fast, creating a roll of gunfire that sent shock waves through the saloon. His bullets crackled into the two men before they could get set and they fell, limbs tangling, in a welter of blood. Morgan squinted through the drifting gunsmoke. No one in the saloon was moving now, and he switched his gaze to Billy Scarfe, standing behind the bar with his hands out of sight beneath it and looking as if he were reaching for a weapon.

'Don't try it, Billy,' Morgan warned, 'or you're dead!'

The 'tender froze. He swallowed nervously, his eyes showing extreme agitation. 'Your gun is empty,' he said in a high-pitched tone. 'I counted your shots. You fired five.'

'Right.' Morgan nodded. 'But I always load six. Go ahead if you think I'm bluffing. But you'll be staking your life on it. I got one shot left, and your name's on it.'

Scarfe's animation seemed to drain out of him. His shoulders slumped and he shook his head. 'Hell, do you reckon I was lifting against you?' he demanded. 'I was coming into it on your side.'

'I don't need any help. Get your hands up and come on out from behind the bar.' Morgan waited until Scarfe had complied, then stepped out from behind the now-stirring Billing and slammed the man up against the bar. He backed off quickly as Billing clung to the bar for support, now shaking his head and striving to regain his composure.

Morgan halted four paces in front of the outlaw, his .44 steady, the muzzle angled slightly, covering the man's heart. 'Jake Billing,' he observed, as if the shooting had not occurred. 'You've changed your appearance some since I last saw you. But I'd know you anywhere. What's brought you into this neck of the woods? It never fails to mystify me how buzzards get word that there are pickings to be had in certain spots. It must be all of five years since you got away from me, Jake. But I knew our trails would cross again some day. Get rid of your gunbelt, and be careful it's only the buckle you touch or you'll be picking lead out of your navel.'

Billing, about forty, tall and wide-shouldered, was badly shocked, his brown eyes filled with uncertainty as he gazed at Morgan's grim figure. He shook his head in disbelief that the one man he feared in the whole West had unexpectedly appeared and got the drop on him. Reaching down, he untied the latigo securing his holster to his right thigh, then unbuckled his gunbelt and let it fall to the floor. The thud of his hardware hitting the pine boards cut through his shock like the knell of doom. He moistened his lips.

'Where in hell did you spring from, Morgan?' he demanded sullenly. 'How long have you been trailing me?'

'He ain't Jake Billing, Morgan,' Scarfe cut in. 'You're making a big mistake. This is Dan Meeker. He's the one who found Wishart lying dead in the bank on the night of the robbery.'

It was Morgan's turn to be shocked. He gazed at Billing while his agile mind digested the information. Then he smiled grimly.

'I would never have believed it,' he mused. 'Jake Billing acting as a bank guard! Now ain't that something? I reckon I don't need to look further for the gang that robbed the bank. You're a snake, Billing, fooling the people around here. But why didn't you run when you got the dough? It ain't like you to stick when you've got what you wanted. Unless there are bigger pickings to be had. Is that it? What are you after?'

Billing shrugged, aware that nothing he said would get him out of this situation. Shock was plain in his eyes. For once in his crooked life he was disconcerted by the turn of events. The one man in the West who could put a rope around his neck had suddenly walked into the saloon with a gun in his hand and got the drop on him. His mind was reeling. He felt as if he were living a nightmare.

Morgan motioned with his gun. 'I guess you know where the jail is, huh? Let's get along there and have a chat about this business. And don't try any tricks or you're dead. I ain't ever gonna forget how you got away from me in Canyon City.'

Billing walked unsteadily to the batwings and Morgan followed closely, his gun lined up on the killer's back. The batwings were thrust open just before Billing reached them and a man wearing a deputy sheriff's badge and holding a pistol entered the saloon. Morgan noted that it was not Mike Bradley.

'Who are you?' Morgan demanded.

'Frank Truscott. It's my day off, but the shooting attracted me. What's going on? I just got back from a spot of fishing.'

'Catch anything?' Morgan grinned when Truscott shook his head. 'You can check the two men over by that upturned table,' he said, 'although I think they're both dead. Then come along to the jail.' He paused. 'Have you heard that the sheriff has been shot?'

'Hell, no! What's been going on around here? And who are you, mister?'

Morgan introduced himself, and Truscott grinned.

'We've been hoping you'd get the wheels turning when you arrived, Morgan,' he said, 'and, by golly, it looks like you've disturbed a hornets' nest.'

Morgan pushed Billing out through the batwings and followed closely. They were trailed at a respectful distance by a growing crowd of townsmen as the astounding news that Dan Meeker was in reality the outlaw Jake Billing spread around the street.

Mike Bradley was sitting at the desk in the law office when Billing walked in on him with the grim figure of Morgan at his back. The deputy, unable to see Morgan's drawn gun, smiled a greeting.

'Howdy, Dan. How you feeling now? I expect you can't wait to get back to work, huh? Say, you're looking a bit peaked.'

'That ain't surprising,' Morgan said. 'Sit down, Billing, in that corner, and remember that it won't be healthy to do more than breathe.'

Bradley saw Morgan's drawn gun and his face changed expression.

'What's going on?' he demanded. 'Have you arrested Dan? What's been happening? I heard the shooting a short time ago but I couldn't leave here because of the prisoners. Cassidy has always stressed that one deputy must remain in the office at all times if we have prisoners in the cells.'

'You know this man as Dan Meeker,' Morgan said. 'But I've arrested Jake Billing, who's wanted in other parts for murder and bank robbery, and I reckon I won't have to look any further for the polecat who planned the bank robbery here. All we want now are the details of what happened that night, and I'm sure Jake will give us the answers we're all eager to learn, like who killed Wishart, where Gus Mulder is, alive or dead, and who else is involved in the dirty business.'

'You're making a big mistake if you reckon I'm the man you want for that job,' Billing rasped. 'No one was more surprised than me when those shots were fired down in the bank. But I didn't have anything to do with it. I was holding down an honest job.'

'You'll have to do better than that.'

Morgan's tone was filled with grim amusement. 'But I guess you're still shocked by your arrest, huh? It came right out of the blue; your worst nightmare coming true. You looked round and there was I with a gun covering you. I never expected it to be that easy, but that's the way it goes, huh? You can't win them all, even though you were pulling your old trick of having a couple of bodyguards watching your back. I overlooked that one, Jake, but it's been a long time. Now let's get down to business. Quit stalling and start talking. I want to know what happened the night Wishart was murdered.'

Billing shook his head and clamped his jaws together. Morgan regarded him for a moment, gauging his attitude, and then nodded.

'We got time on our side, Jake,' he said. 'We've also jailed some of the men I think were in your plot to rob the bank. When I get statements from them it should be easy to work out what happened.'

'I wasn't in it.' Billing shook his head

obstinately. 'You got me for those charges you made five years ago, Morgan, but they won't stand up in court now. If you live long enough, you'll see me walk free as a bird.'

'Let's put him behind bars and give him time to sweat,' Morgan suggested. 'I got some more checking-out to do before I settle down to some serious questioning. Let's make sure none of these men can talk together to get their stories right, huh? Get up and turn out your pockets, Billing. We might find something incriminating on you. It just ain't your day, is it?'

Billing obeyed wordlessly and Morgan checked the few articles that came to light, finding nothing incriminating. Bradley picked up the cell keys and they escorted Billing into the cell block, lodging him in a cell at the far end of the passage. Morgan watched the outlaw throw himself down on the bunk in the cell and put his hands behind his head. Billing grinned defiantly, but Morgan could see worry in the man's sharp gaze. He turned away, feeling good for the first time since his arrival in Turkey Creek. The mystery of what had happened on the night of Wishart's murder could not remain secret much longer.

Frank Truscott came into the office as Morgan and Bradley returned to it.

'Hi, Frank,' Bradley greeted. 'Catch anything? You certainly picked the right day to be off duty this week. Have we had developments! This is Cleef Morgan, the Pinkerton man we've been expecting.'

'We've met.' Truscott grinned. 'I've arranged for Mort Joiner to take care of the two men lying dead in the saloon. How's the sheriff? Is he badly hurt? Nobody in town seems to know anything worth a damn.'

'He'll be on his feet in a couple of weeks,' Bradley said.

'Let's look at what we have now,' Morgan cut in. 'I think we've got the man in custody who is behind the robbery here. He's a notorious outlaw in the north. So while he was here, who has he been associating with? There were two hardcases in the saloon when I braced him, and there must be others in the gang he works with. I used to know all the members of his gang, but I killed most of them five years ago so he'll have formed a new bunch now.'

'There ain't many men he socialized with,' Bradley mused. 'He was always a loner, it seemed to me.'

'What about Mull Johnson?' asked Truscott. 'Him and Meeker always had their heads together whenever I saw them. They were quite thick, which surprised me, because Johnson is a big bozo with rocks in his head. But he was Meeker's fetch-and-carry man, paid to run Meeker's errands.'

'You can talk to him, but I doubt you'll get any sense out of Johnson,' Bradley opined. He looked at Morgan. 'Johnson got thrown off a horse when he was young and fell on his head. He never makes much sense. Don't get side-tracked with Johnson. You've got something going now, and with a little luck you'll crack this mystery.'

'Do you know where I'll find Johnson at this time?' Morgan asked. 'I want to search Meeker's room at the boarding-house to see what I can turn up, and I might be able to get something from Johnson.'

'I'll go with you,' Truscott said. 'I want to be in at the end of this. Over the past five weeks I've racked my brains trying to work out what might have happened.'

'I've said all along that it had to be someone who was playing poker in the apartment over the bank that night,' Bradley volunteered.

'Will you be all right here now your jail is about filled with prisoners?' Morgan queried.

Bradley nodded. 'Ike Sayer will be coming on duty presently. He's the night jailer when we've got prisoners in.'

Morgan nodded and departed. He

still had plenty to do. Truscott went with him and they walked to Ma Templeton's boardinghouse. There was the smell of supper cooking, and Ma Templeton confronted them when they entered.

'I'm afraid Dan hasn't returned yet,' she informed Morgan.

'That's all right. I've seen him, and he's staying with us tonight.' Morgan smiled. 'I need to take a look around his room, if you wouldn't mind.'

'I'll take you up there.' Ma Templeton produced a bunch of keys. 'Dan is a very private man. He always keeps his room locked. But as you're a law officer I'm sure he would not object to me letting you look around.' She led the way up to the room and unlocked the door, then backed away. 'I'll be down in my kitchen if there's anything else you want.'

Morgan nodded and entered the room. Truscott remained in the doorway, watching with interest while Morgan went through the room thoroughly.

'I didn't expect to find anything,' Morgan said at length. 'Billing wouldn't be so stupid as to leave something incriminating in here. So let's find Johnson and see what he can tell us.'

'He's got the mind of a boy,' Truscott warned. 'But he's mighty dangerous when he's likkered up and rarin' to go. It usually takes three of us to get him into a cell. He sleeps in the hayloft over the stable, and that's where we'll probably find him.'

'The hayloft, huh?' Morgan's mind flitted back over the incidents that had occurred since he rode into Turkey Creek. 'Did you know a man was stabbed to death in the stable earlier this afternoon?'

'No!' Truscott was shocked, and Morgan went on to relate what had happened. 'Jeez, it gets worse and worse,' the deputy remarked. 'Are you thinking that Johnson might have done it?'

'That's what I'm hoping to find out.'

Morgan led the way down the stairs

and they went out to the street. Night had closed in now, and heavy shadows lay around them as they traversed the sidewalk to the livery barn at the other end of town.

There was a single lantern burning in the doorway of the barn. Truscott lifted it from its nail and held it high as he went inside. Morgan followed, his hand down on the butt of his holstered gun. He wrinkled his nose at the sharp ammoniac smell of horses within.

'Hey, Johnson, are you up there?' Truscott called, halting at the foot of the ladder leading up to the loft, and they stood in heavy silence, listening for a reply. Moments elapsed and, when there was no response, Truscott tut-tutted and started to ascend the ladder, carrying the lantern in his left hand, then hanging it on a hook fixed to the underside of the loft floor. He had almost reached the loft when Morgan became aware of straws spiralling down upon him.

'Someone is up there,' he warned.

Truscott halted and looked up. 'Johnson, this is Frank, the deputy. Come on down. I need to talk to you.'

'I ain't done nothing,' came a growled reply from the darkness above.

'I ain't wanting you for anything, Mull. I need to talk to you, that's all.' The deputy sounded as if he was humouring a wilful child.

'I ain't feeling good for talking now. In the morning will be better.'

'This won't wait until the morning,' Morgan responded. 'It'll only take a few minutes. We got a lot of things to do around town before morning, and you could help us.'

'Who's that with you, Frank?' The voice became suspicious, rising sharply.

'It's the Pinkerton man everyone's been waiting for,' Truscott said. 'Come on, Mull. We only want to talk to you. Show yourself and I'll let you wear my badge while we're talking.'

Morgan, gazing up into the shadows, saw movement, and the next instant a bale of hay came plunging down through the trap, striking Truscott, taking him unawares, and both bale and deputy came crashing to the ground. A jeering laugh sounded from the loft.

'I told you I don't wanta talk,' Johnson said, 'and I ain't gonna.'

Morgan bent over Trustcott, who was groaning, and pulled the bale of hay off him.

'You all right?' he demanded.

'I don't think anything is broken.' Truscott moved his arms and legs gingerly before getting to his feet. He staggered and almost fell as he picked up his hat and knocked it back into shape before replacing it on his head. 'It looks like we're not gonna have any luck with Johnson tonight,' he opined.

'Stay down here and watch out for more bales,' Morgan said. He turned to the ladder and ascended swiftly until his head was level with the floor of the loft. 'Mull Johnson,' he called. 'I could do with some help in this case I'm handling, and I'll give you three dollars if you can help me.'

'Three dollars?' There was a pause. 'Give me the money first.'

'Sure. Come on down. We've got a deal.' Morgan backed down the ladder, and by the time he reached the ground a big man was descending with practised ease.

Johnson's feet hit the ground hard and he turned to face the two lawmen, an inane grin on his slack mouth. He was almost as tall as Morgan, nearly as big, and was probably in his middle twenties. Lamplight put glints in his narrowed brown eyes, and there was a leering expression on his fleshy face. He was wearing a red-check shirt, ragged pants, and old riding-boots that someone had evidently thrown away. The left boot had a circular piece of leather cut out of it at the spot where it could relieve the pressure of a bunion at the base of the big toe. A shapeless, weather-stained black Stetson with a torn brim was pushed back on his head, revealing dark curly hair that was badly in need of a wash. Sticking out a big hand, he waggled his fingers.

'Gimme the three dollars,' he said.

Morgan reached into his pocket and produced some change. He handed over three dollars, and Johnson tested them with his teeth before nodding. Morgan held up an extra dollar.

'I'll give you this as well, if you can tell me what I want to know,' he enticed.

Johnson snatched at the dollar but Morgan was too quick for him. Johnson's expression changed quickly and ill humour showed in his dark eyes.

'You can have it when you've told me what you know,' Morgan said firmly. 'How long have you been in the stable today? I need to know about some of the people who were in here this afternoon.'

'I ain't never left the stable. I work here for three dollars a week, taking care of the horses and mucking out. I've got a mountain of muck out back.'

'Can you remember what you did today?' Morgan pursued. 'Did you eat at noon?'

'Sure did. Never miss chuck. But they don't let me sit in the eating-house. I have to eat out back.'

'What did you do after eating?'

'Swept out the stable. Mr Ashby looksees every afternoon. He gets real angry if I ain't swept the place. If I don't do like he says then I don't get paid, even if I've done the work.'

'So you swept the stable. How long did that take?'

'Till it's done. I don't know how long it takes. I ain't got a watch. I don't have to tell them how long I take. They tell me what to do and I get on with it.'

Johnson's tone had risen to a dangerous high by the time he finished speaking, and Truscott lifted a placating hand.

'Don't ruffle your feathers, Mull,' he said easily. 'Think of that other dollar.'

'Well what are you getting at? Are you saying I don't spend enough time on my chores? Mr Ashby is satisfied, and he's the boss.'

'I'm trying to establish what you were

179

doing at a certain time,' Morgan said patiently. 'Did many folks come in here around the time you were sweeping?'

'Yeah. People are coming in an' out all the time.'

'Who, for instance?' Morgan flipped the extra dollar into the air and caught it deftly. Johnson followed the spinning coin with intent gaze and Morgan flipped the dollar again, this time towards Johnson, who displayed remarkable speed intercepting it.

'Who did you see, Mull?' Morgan persisted. 'Name all the people who showed up here this afternoon. It's very important. Don't miss anyone.'

'Mr Ashby. He came. Like I said, he looks to see I'm doing my jobs. Mike Bradley and that nice Mattie Scarfe gal came. They always go up in the loft. Mike gave me money so I don't tell anyone I've seen them.'

'Did you see Cass Frayne?' Morgan demanded.

'Frayne?' Johnson shook his head. 'I don't know that name. I guess he must be a stranger in town.'

'Did you see a stranger this afternoon? He came in and collected a knife in his chest. Did you stab him, Johnson?'

Johnson's expression changed. He backed off warily. Alarm sparked to life in his eyes. He shook his head.

'It wasn't me stuck him,' he protested. 'Dan was here talking when a man I didn't know came in the back door and started shouting. Dan told him to stop shouting. The man pulled a gun, and Dan got him in the chest with a knife. Dan didn't start it. He went out the back door and I went up into the loft by the back ladder. I hid in the straw. After Dan went I saw the man with the knife in his chest get up and go out the front door.'

'Who's Dan, Mull?' Truscott asked. 'Has he got a second name?'

'Yeah. Dan Meeker. He's my friend. He likes me. I swore I wouldn't tell anyone what happened. Dan said he would get angry if I did. You won't tell

Dan I told you, will you, mister? I wouldn't want him to be angry with me.'

'It'll be all right.' Morgan glanced at Truscott. 'Let's get back to the jail. I reckon I've got enough now to open up this case. You get on with your work, Mull.' He patted the big man's shoulder. 'You've done fine, just fine.'

'You won't tell Dan I told you about the stranger, will you?' Johnson asked fearfully. 'I never saw a knife-throw like Dan's, and it was the knife I found that Dan used. It hit that stranger dead centre faster than I could see it. But the man asked for it. He shouted at Dan, then pulled a gun on him.'

'So you found the knife, huh, Mull?' Morgan asked. 'Where did you pick it up?'

'Right here in the stable. It was a couple of days ago. I gave it to Dan. He was here when I found it.'

Morgan nodded and turned abruptly to leave the stable. He strode resolutely along the sidewalk, his mind filled with the salient points of his investigation. A pattern was beginning to emerge from the welter of detail he had garnered through his questions, and he fitted the information from Mull Johnson into the shape that was evolving. As he reached the front of the hotel he paused, thinking of Jenny Mulder, aware that he was not happy with what she had said to him earlier. He looked at Truscott, who stood patiently at his side.

'Go on to the law office,' Morgan said. 'There's something else I got to do before I can ease off. I'll be a few minutes, that's all. Then we'll start grilling the prisoners. See you at the jail, huh?'

'Sure thing.' Truscott went on along the sidewalk.

Morgan watched the deputy until he had reached the door of the law office, and went into the hotel as Truscott disappeared off the street. He approached the reception desk, where Amos Henty was seated, reading a magazine. The clerk looked up at

Morgan's approach and his expression filled with alarm when he saw the detective. He glanced quickly at the stairs and, following the little man's turn of the head, Morgan was surprised to see Jenny Mulder appearing, accompanied by two tough-looking men. One was leading the way, a gun ready in his hand. The other was grasping the girl's right arm, thrusting her down the stairs much faster than she normally travelled.

8

Morgan dropped to one knee as the first shot was fired. He angled the muzzle of his gun upwards slightly as a bullet crackled by his left ear, then fired. The foremost man on the stairs jerked and folded at the waist before toppling down to ground level, his pistol falling from suddenly nerveless fingers. The man grasping Jenny's arm dropped a hand to his holstered gun, and the girl lunged against him as he drew swiftly, throwing him off balance. Morgan lifted his muzzle, but stayed his hand because Jenny was in the line of fire. The next instant a heavy object crashed against Morgan's head and darkness enveloped him. The carpet seemed to come up and hit him in the face and he relaxed into unconsciousness.

When he opened his eyes again he

found Frank Truscott bending over him. The hotel lobby was filled with men asking questions. Morgan looked around, saw a dead man lying at the foot of the stairs, then looked for Amos Henty, wincing as he did so. But the little hotel clerk was absent from his desk, which was what Morgan expected.

'What happened?' Truscott demanded.

'Where's Jenny Mulder?' Morgan countered.

'I ain't seen her.' The deputy shook his head as he helped Morgan to his feet. He picked up the detective's gun and stuck it back into Morgan's holster.

Morgan put a hand to his aching head. 'Get these men out of here,' he rapped, and moved to a seat beside the desk. Slumping down heavily, he closed his eyes as a wave of nausea filled him, and sight and sound diminished as his senses whirled.

Truscott moved quickly, pushing men towards the door. Morgan waited until the lobby was cleared before rising. He staggered, and Truscott grasped his left arm to steady him. Morgan explained what had happened, and Truscott nodded.

'I ran out of the office when I heard the shots,' he said, 'and saw several horses coming out of the alley opposite. They crossed the street to the front of the hotel and stopped. I reckon there were five broncs — three of them riderless. It was too dark to pick out details, but a couple of figures came out of here, mounted up, and they all rode away out of town.'

'Jenny Mulder has been taken, and against her will, it looks like.' Morgan went to the stairs and stood over the body. 'Any idea who this is?' he demanded.

'Yeah.' Truscott nodded. 'It's Hap Denton, one of Ashby's riders from S Bar A.'

'Ashby, huh? Let's go talk to him. And it looks like Henty has sloped off. It had to be him who hit me. He was at the desk and I turned my back on him when the two men came down the stairs with Jenny.'

'It won't be too difficult to run Henty down,' Truscott said. 'He didn't come out of here after the shooting. He's probably skulking in one of the rooms.'

Morgan drew his gun and checked the cylinder. He refilled an empty chamber. His eyes were narrowed as he strode out of the hotel and made for the saloon, staggering twice on the sidewalk as his senses whirled disconcertingly. But he kept moving, thrust through the batwings of the saloon and walked to the bar to confront Mattie Scarfe, who was serving alongside her father.

'Is Ashby around?' Morgan demanded.

Billy Scarfe pushed his daughter aside and stepped in front of Morgan. 'You look like you could do with a drink,' he observed.

Morgan shook his head, and winced at the movement. 'All I want right now is Ashby.'

'He'll be in his office. You want I

should get him?'

'I'll get him.' Morgan strode to the door leading to the rear of the saloon with Truscott following closely. Morgan knocked at the door of the office and Ashby called out an invitation to enter. As he thrust the door open, Morgan saw Ashby at his desk with Jonas Draper seated beside it. They were drinking, and Ashby was refilling their glasses.

Draper sprang up when he saw Morgan, then set down his glass and turned to leave.

'I got to be going, Sam,' he said. 'I'll drop by in the morning.'

'Stay where you are,' Morgan snapped, and the little lawyer froze in his tracks.

'What the hell do you want?' Ashby demanded. 'You got no right to come busting in here. I find your attitude too damn high-handed for honest folk.'

'I've just killed Hap Denton,' Morgan said. 'He drew on me when I walked in on him and one of his pards taking Jenny Mulder out of the hotel against her will.'

'The hell you say!' Ashby's face paled.

'Is that all you can say?' Morgan demanded.

'Where is Jenny now?' Draper ventured, stuttering in his nervousness.

Truscott explained what he had seen, and Morgan nodded grimly as Ashby met his gaze.

'Don't tell me you didn't know what was happening,' Morgan said. 'They were your men, and you must know what is going on.'

'As God is my witness,' Ashby began, then, seeing the expression that came to Morgan's face, his voice trailed off. He shrugged his shoulders in hopelessness and leaned back in his seat. 'I guess you won't listen to anything I got to say,' he said resignedly.

'I'm always ready to listen to the truth,' Morgan responded. 'You may not think I'm making any progress in my investigation, but you better know I'm getting there, slowly but surely. So if there's anything on your mind you reckon I ought to know about then spit it out. It'll be easier if you tell me rather than if I have to force it out of you.'

Ashby looked at the silent Draper, who was standing motionless. The lawyer's face was pale, his hands trembling uncontrollably. There was fear in his expression, coupled with defeat, and Morgan fancied that a good session of questioning would break the lawyer. He fought against impatience, aware that the momentum of the case would get him through.

'Jonas, you're an attorney, for God's sake,' Ashby said furiously. 'Get this man off my back. I've been trying to get law and order into this town for years, and the minute a detective shows up I turn out to be his prime suspect.'

'There's nothing I can do until the truth comes out.' Draper shook his head. 'I think I'm under suspicion myself.'

'And why shouldn't you be?' Morgan rapped. 'Two men attacked me earlier as I left the saloon, and when I accused you of setting them on to me you said you knew they were out to get me, but you didn't say who was responsible for them. Would you care to enlighten me now?'

Draper shook his head. 'I don't know a damn thing about any of this! If I did, and told you about it, I'd probably disappear like Gus Mulder did.'

'Let's all go along to the jail,' Morgan decided. 'You two can spend the night behind bars on suspicion of being involved in this crooked business.' He glanced at Truscott. 'Do you feel up to a ride at this time of the day?'

'Sure thing.' The deputy nodded without hesitation. 'Where to?'

'Ashby's ranch. His men took Jenny Mulder, and I guess we know where they've gone. How far out of town is S Bar A?'

'About seven miles.' Truscott sounded eager. 'You want I should saddle our horses?'

'If you would. My brown stallion is in the third stall on the right. I'll take these two along to the jail. Bring three horses. Ashby is gonna ride with us.'

Truscott nodded and departed. Morgan looked at Ashby and the discomfited Draper.

'If either of you two is armed then now is the time to declare it,' he said.

Ashby unbuttoned his jacket and showed Morgan the butt of a small pistol in a shoulder holster. Morgan relieved him of the weapon and gazed at Draper.

'I never carry a gun,' Draper said.

'Then let's get on with it. You know where the jail is. Get moving.'

The two men did not argue, and Morgan followed them out of the saloon and along to the law office. Mike Bradley looked up when they entered the office, and gazed enquiringly at Morgan.

'Draper is gonna spend the night with you, Mike,' Morgan said. 'You can hold him on suspicion of being involved in the bank robbery. Ashby is riding out to his spread with Truscott and me.'

'So you're calling the shots now,' Bradley observed. 'Can you make anything stick against these two? They're slippery as a mud hole.'

'I've got a little going for me.' Morgan considered his next move. 'You got any objection to riding out to your place with me, Ashby? If you're innocent then you'll be keen to learn why your outfit is in the kidnapping business without your knowledge.'

'Anything you say,' Ashby replied tonelessly. 'You don't believe me so I'd better go with you. I want to be there when you discover I'm innocent.'

'What about you, Draper?' Morgan turned his attention to the lawyer. 'Are you still pushing that innocent stuff?'

'I don't have to answer your questions,' Draper said primly.

Bradley took the lawyer into the cell block and locked him in a cell. Morgan motioned Ashby to a seat and stood over him.

'I've got a picture of what happened on the night of the bank robbery,'

194

Morgan said. 'Dan Meeker is behind bars. It turns out that he is Jake Billing, the outlaw. I arrested him for bank robbery and murder about five years ago but he got away from me. Now I find he's been working here in Turkey Creek as a bank guard, of all things. So I don't need to look any further for my bank robber. Billing organized it, and I've jailed the men I think helped him do the job. I've recovered three thousand dollars of the stolen money, and there are only a few gaps to fill in before I can pin the guilt where it belongs. I even got the man who knifed your pet gunman, Cass Frayne. Do you still deny that you brought Frayne into town?'

'I never heard of the man.' Ashby shook his head. 'I'd like to know what I'd want with a gunman. I run several businesses around here, and I don't get trouble from anyone. You're barking up the wrong tree, mister.'

'Sure, if you say so, but I got a

witness who says different.' Morgan grinned.

'Who in hell is that?' Ashby paused, but Morgan remained silent. 'Someone who's jealous of me, I shouldn't wonder,' Ashby mused. 'You better be sure of your evidence before you take it into court, Mister Detective.'

The street door opened and Frank Truscott looked into the office as Bradley returned from the cells to hang a bunch of keys on a nail in the wall behind the desk. Morgan tapped Ashby on the shoulder and the man got to his feet.

'We'll be back in the morning,' Morgan told Bradley, and ushered Ashby out of the office.

Morgan was greatly relieved when they were astride their horses and riding out of town. He needed time in which to think about the developments that had occurred, and this trip was the perfect respite. He mulled over incidents as they rode. Ashby rode between them in Indian file, with Truscott ahead to lead Morgan to the ranch. The night was starry, with a half-moon showing high in the south, The range looked ghostly and unreal in the silvery shadows, and a faintly perfumed breeze blew into their faces.

They were a silent trio as they cantered over the rough ground. The miles slipped by, and soon Truscott was reining in and turning in his saddle.

'The ranch is just ahead,' he informed Morgan. 'If we ride any closer they might hear us, and if they have brought Jenny Mulder here they'll be expecting pursuit. Shall we walk the rest of the way?'

'Yeah.' Morgan dismounted and tied his reins to a bush. 'Ashby, you stick close by me, and if you make a sound it'll probably be your last. Frank, keep an eye on Ashby at all times. We'll play this game as she comes. The object is to locate Jenny Mulder, and if we find she's here we'll handle it accordingly. Now, point me in the direction of the spread.'

'I wanta see your face when you learn

I'm innocent,' Ashby said.

Morgan went on ahead, and when he reached the top of a slope he saw the lights of a ranch house just ahead, with a separate lamp to the left, marking the position of a bunkhouse. He walked swiftly, angling to reach the right-hand corner of the house, his feet making no sound in the grass. When he reached the house he paused to look around, peering along the veranda, where lamplight speared through the shadows from two windows. He motioned for Ashby to remain beyond the corner, and Truscott stood behind the town mayor.

Morgan stepped on to the veranda and eased in close to the nearest lighted window. Flattening against the wall and staying out of the lamplight, he craned forward to peer into a long room where three men were seated around one end of a long table. They were playing cards. Morgan's eyes glinted when he saw Jenny Mulder seated in an easy-chair in front of an empty fireplace, staring into space, her hands and feet bound tightly.

For long moments he gazed at the hapless girl, then eased off the veranda and went back around the corner. He grasped the motionless Ashby by his shirt front and almost lifted the man off his feet, thrusting him against the wall of the house.

'So you're innocent, are you?' he demanded in an undertone. 'So now tell me there's something wrong with my eyes and that Jenny Mulder ain't sitting hogtied inside with three men guarding her.'

'I don't believe you,' Ashby said.

'We'll soon get the truth of it,' Morgan replied. 'How many riders do you employ here?'

'Five. Let me take a look at the men. I don't know what's going on here, Morgan, I swear it. I have a ranch foreman running the place. I never come out here. I'm always too busy to leave town. If my crew are playing some deep game themselves then I want to know about it. Let's go in and confront them.'

'That's what I'm planning to do,' Morgan said grimly. 'But you're gonna stay out of it. Frank, there's a light in that bunkhouse window. If there's shooting inside the house when I go in then you make sure nobody gets at me from behind. If you have to challenge anyone then make it loud and clear that you are the law. You got that?'

'Sure enough, and I'll keep an eye on Ashby,' Truscott replied.

Morgan palmed his gun, checked it, then returned to the veranda, catfooting along to the front door, which opened to his touch. He entered the house silently and closed the door softly, standing with his back to it in a passage that reached through to the back of the building. A single lamp was burning on a small table to the right. There was a flight of stairs to the left, and several doors opened off the passage. He went to the first door on the right and paused for a moment, drawing a deep breath as he steadied himself. Then he opened the door and stepped boldly into the room.

The door creaked, attracting the attention of the three men at the table. One of them reacted instantly, thrusting back his chair and rising, reaching for a holstered gun despite the fact that Morgan's pistol was in full view and levelled.

'Leave it be,' Morgan rapped.

The man paused, seemed to freeze, and then continued his draw. Morgan fired a shot that sent thunderous echoes through the house and the night. His bullet hit the man in the chest. He twisted away and fell heavily to the floor, his gun flying from his hand. Morgan stepped away from the door, covering the other two, who were motionless with their hands in plain view. Out of the corner of his eye, Morgan could see Jenny Mulder gazing at him, shocked by his sudden appearance. Her mouth was open but no sound emanated from it. Then her astonishment receded, and a long cry of relief escaped her as she recognized him.

'On your feet,' Morgan rapped, and the two men arose, lifting their hands shoulder-high. He walked around the table and disarmed them, throwing their weapons the length of the long room. One of the men had taken Jenny out of the hotel. He tapped the man on the shoulder with the barrel of his gun. 'Untie Miss Mulder,' he said.

At that instant several shots were fired outside, sending echoes hammering over the spread. The door of the room opened quickly and a man armed with a rifle burst in, his face showing urgency and fear. The shooting outside was not repeated. Echoes were fading slowly.

'Say, what's all the shooting about?' the newcomer demanded, and began turning his rifle on Morgan, who was covering him.

'Drop it,' Morgan rapped.

The man paused, then let go of his rifle and raised his hands. He indicated the pistol in the holster on his right hip and Morgan motioned for him to get rid of it. The man did so, then stood gazing down at the dead man on the floor. When she was freed, Jenny Mulder stood up and rubbed her wrists. Morgan backed to the nearest window overlooking the porch and opened it with his left hand.

'Frank,' he called. 'What's happening out there?'

'No trouble,' came the reply. 'A couple of men came running from the bunkhouse when you cut loose inside. I challenged them but they didn't want to know so I dropped them. They're both dead. Ashby says they're not his crew.'

'Bring Ashby in here,' Morgan directed. He looked at the girl, who appeared to be badly shocked. 'Care to tell me what this is all about, Miss Mulder?' he asked. 'When I saw you at the hotel you seemed to be in a lot of trouble.'

'I don't know what is going on,

really,' she replied, shaking her head. She indicated the man Morgan had recognized. 'He came to my room in the hotel and said he would take me to my father, claiming that Dad is alive and being held prisoner. I decided to go with him, then changed my mind because it all seemed too suspicious. I wanted to see you, but he turned nasty and forced me to go along with him.' She shrugged. 'You know the rest of it. You shot one of them and then Amos Henty hit you from behind and I was rushed out of the hotel. They had horses ready, and brought me here. I've been hogtied ever since.'

Morgan nodded. He heard footsteps coming into the house, and then Frank Truscott called to him. Ashby stepped into the doorway and the deputy followed him into the room. Morgan ordered the three men to sit down at the table and motioned for Truscott to guard them from the rear. He pointed to a chair at the head of the table.

'Sit there, Ashby,' he said, and the

man obeyed, his face set grimly. 'Is there anyone else in the house?' he demanded, his gaze on the man he had seen taking Jenny out of the hotel. 'You tell me,' he added.

'There's no one else.' The man shrugged. 'We were just having a bit of fun.'

'You'll have to do better than that,' Morgan warned. 'Let's get down to it. Why was Miss Mulder taken from the hotel and brought here?'

The man remained silent, staring at the table top, his expression sullen. Morgan let his gaze rove over the faces of the other men. None would meet his gaze, and he turned his attention to the grim-faced Ashby.

'And I suppose you're going to say you know nothing about this, huh?' He held up a hand as Ashby opened his mouth to reply. 'Frank, check out the house. Someone might be skulking about.'

The deputy nodded and departed. Morgan pointed at Ashby.

'Go on,' he invited. 'What have you got to say?'

'Sprague, tell me the truth,' Ashby said. 'I put you in charge of running this place. Why did you take Jenny Mulder from the hotel and bring her here?'

'I got nothing to say,' the man replied, then set his jaw and refused to say more.

'I'm under suspicion of being involved in this,' Ashby continued, 'so talk, damn you! Tell this detective what he wants to know.'

'Is Gus Mulder alive?' Morgan pressed.

'I don't know.' Sprague shook his head. 'I ain't seen him since before the bank robbery. I told you, what we did was just a bit of fun.'

Morgan could hear footsteps descending the stairs and covered the doorway with his gun. Truscott appeared, grinning.

'Look who I found hogtied upstairs,' he said and stepped aside out of the doorway.

A tall man appeared. He was heavily bearded, his eyes blinking rapidly in the lamplight. He was rubbing his wrists and shrugging his shoulders as if his body was cramped. Jenny sprang to her feet and ran to him.

'Dad!' she cried, hurling herself into his arms. Her sobbing was muffled by the big man's broad shoulder.

Morgan watched, his mind busy. So Gus Mulder was not dead. He nodded slowly, aware that this development just about ended the case. He waited, and there was heavy silence in the room. Jenny turned to Morgan, her face tear-streaked, her eyes shining.

Ashby sprang up from the table and hurried towards Mulder, grasping the rancher's hand and shaking it furiously.

'I'm glad you're alive, Gus,' he said. 'Where have you been for the last five weeks? Everyone thought you were dead. So what happened when you went down into the bank with Wishart that night we were playing cards? Everyone believed you killed Wishart and committed the robbery. For God's sake, tell us what really happened.'

'I don't rightly know.' Mulder put a hand to his eyes. 'I followed Wishart down the stairs into the bank and someone hit me on the head from behind. When I came to I was lying face down across a saddle, hogtied, and being taken across the range in the night. There were several riders around, and I was brought here, where I've been held prisoner ever since. Sprague was running this business. He told me the bank had been robbed and Wishart was dead. He insisted that folk believed I'd done the robbery and got away with the money. Then that weasel Jonas Draper turned up. He came several times over the past month, and each time he tried to talk me into signing away my ranch.'

'So that was it.' Morgan nodded. 'I had a feeling your ranch was behind it although at first I believed you to be dead. And Jenny seemed to be under pressure to sell. I thought Hank Whiteman might be at the back of it.

But come and sit down and relax. I'm Cleef Morgan, a Pinkerton detective handling the case of Wishart's murder and the bank robbery. We'll go over what happened to you step by step until we get the rights of it.'

'It's been a nightmare,' Mulder said, walking around the table. He paused behind Sprague's chair and grasped the man by the shoulders, hauling him out of the seat and hitting him on the jaw with a powerful right-hand punch. 'You could have treated me better,' he declared. 'I owe you a lot for the past month.'

Sprague fell to the floor and Mulder kicked him. Ashby rushed forward and grasped his dazed foreman, hauled him to his feet, and invited Mulder to hit him again.

'Lay off the rough stuff,' Morgan directed. 'Stick Sprague back in his seat and then you can all sit down.' He waited until they complied. Jenny sat beside her father and held his arm as if afraid he would suddenly disappear.

'That's better.' Morgan viewed the intent faces watching him. Sprague was hunched forward, his elbows on the table, his head supported on his hands. Mulder was massaging his temples. 'Who else showed up here while you were being held?' Morgan asked Mulder.

'I didn't see anyone else.' Mulder shook his head. 'It's as big a mystery to me as to the rest of you. Each time I asked Draper who it was wanted my spread he told me I didn't need to know. I've had plenty of time to think since that night, but I got no idea who is behind it.'

'Then let's talk to the man who must know,' Morgan said grimly, transferring his attention to Sprague. 'Who do you take your orders from, Sprague? If it isn't Ashby then name your real boss.'

'Hold it,' Truscott cut in. 'I can hear a rider coming into the yard.'

Morgan reacted with his customary presence of mind. He moved to the door of the room with long strides.

'Keep everyone quiet in here, Frank,' he said in passing the deputy. 'I'll welcome our visitor.'

Truscott nodded. Morgan went out to the porch and stood in dense shadows to one side of the door, his back to the wall of the house. He cocked his gun as his narrowed eyes picked out the dim figure of an approaching rider, and readied himself for action . . .

9

The rider galloping across the yard to the ranch house brought his mount to a dust-raising halt in front of the veranda and flung himself out of leather almost before the horse had stopped. Leaving his reins trailing, he came on to the veranda with tinkling spurs.

'Hold it right there,' Morgan rasped, stepping forward into lamplight which was reflected from his levelled pistol. 'You're covered. Who are you? What's your business?'

The man halted and lifted his hands away from his belt.

'I'm looking for Morgan, the Pinkerton detective. Is he here?'

'You're talking to him. What's the trouble?'

'Mike Bradley sent me. He's got big trouble in town. About ten men are trying to shoot their way into the jail.

We think Buck Whiteman is bossing them. I'm Ike Sayer, the night jailer. I'd just got into the law office on duty when the raiders showed up. Bradley sent me out the back door with orders to come and tell you.'

'Come into the house.' Morgan stepped aside for Sayer to precede him. The night jailer walked into the big room and Truscott called a greeting.

'Ike, what in blazes are you doing here?'

Sayer repeated his message and there was instant concern from Mulder and Ashby.

'I'll ride into town,' Mulder said. He had armed himself with two of the pistols that had been discarded by his former captors.

'I'll go with you,' Ashby added.

'Hold it,' Morgan intervened. 'I'll be hot-footing it back to town, and I think Frank should go with me.'

'I'll be riding back pronto,' Sayer cut in. 'Bradley is on his own in the jail, and I doubt if any of the townsmen will go to his aid. Nobody has ever made a stand against the Whitemans. They ride roughshod over anyone who gets in their way.'

'If you've just flogged your horse over seven miles then you won't be able to keep up with me,' Morgan said. 'Do like I say. You and Mulder can bring these prisoners into town. Tie them to their saddles, and don't lose anyone. They've been caught in the act of breaking the law and I need their testimony to complete my case.'

'What about me?' Ashby demanded.

Morgan regarded the town mayor for a moment, then nodded. 'You can ride with me, and you better be on the level. Come on, let's get moving.'

Truscott made for the door and Ashby followed him closely. Morgan called to Truscott:

'Fetch the horses here to the house. By the time you return I'll have these sidewinders tied and ready to travel. Sayer, go and saddle up horses for the trip. Mulder, keep your gun on these men and I'll rope them.'

'We can handle them,' Sayer said, drawing his gun. 'I am a deputy, so I'll take over here. Just let these bozos try something, that's all. Bradley will be needing all the help he can get. The jail is built like a fort and he should be able to hold out long enough for you to get back, but don't waste more time than you have to.'

Morgan nodded and departed quickly. He hurried through the night to where the horses had been left, and arrived at the spot as Truscott sprang into his saddle. Morgan mounted his brown stallion and swung in beside Truscott and they went hammering through the night back to town with Ashby following closely.

The moon was high in a cloudless sky, but the surrounding shadows were deceptive as they galloped resolutely through the night. Ashby began to drop back. Morgan noticed the fact but ignored it, although he kept glancing over his shoulder. Ashby seemed to be making efforts to stay up with them but his horse was not good enough. When the lights of Turkey Creek showed, Morgan glanced backwards yet again, and saw no sign of Ashby.

Gun flashes were splitting the shadows in town. Red-and-orange muzzle flame speared through the night as gun thunder came rolling and echoing across the range. Morgan spurred his mount and the big animal lengthened its stride and pulled ahead of Truscott's horse.

When he reached the end of the street, Morgan could pick out the positions of the guns firing into the office. There were four guns opposite the jail keeping up a steady rate of fire, and he could hear weapons hammering at the rear of the building. He pulled his horse to the right and rode into an alley. He dismounted swiftly and palmed his .44. Truscott arrived as Morgan peered out of the alley, and the deputy rode by, his gun flaming as he spurred towards the attackers.

Morgan cursed and went into the fight at a run. Two of the attackers had turned their weapons on Truscott, and Morgan winced when the deputy's horse crashed to the ground, but Truscott rolled clear. A bullet crackled past Morgan's left ear. He started shooting, aiming for gun flashes. When he reached Truscott's horse he saw the deputy pushing himself erect, his gun booming defiantly.

Morgan ducked as a slug snarled at him from the darkened window of the law office. He fired at a gun flash emanating from an alley just ahead, exactly opposite the jail, and saw a figure detach itself from the shadows and sprawl into the street. There was only one gun firing now from the main street and, as he aimed at it, the attacker ceased firing. Echoes rolled heavily away across the town until an uneasy silence settled.

Truscott came to Morgan's side, reloading his pistol. The shooting at the rear of the jail had ceased. Somewhere in the background, several dogs were barking furiously. Morgan moistened his lips, and tasted gunsmoke on them.

'Looks like we got here in time,' Truscott observed. He raised his voice. 'Mike, it's Truscott and Morgan out here. We're coming into the office.'

'Come ahead,' Bradley replied.

Morgan turned to one of the prostrate attackers and carried him as they crossed the street, watching their surroundings. The office door swung open as they reached it. The office was in darkness, the interior filled with gunsmoke.

'Glad to see you,' Bradley said from the darkness. 'You didn't waste any time getting back. It was a close thing here. Jack Santee came in after Ike Sayer left for Ashby's place, just before that gang cut me off from help. He fought them off at the back and I handled the street out front. How did it go at Ashby's?'

'Where is Ashby?' Truscott cut in.

'He dropped back and finally took

off,' Morgan said. 'But he'll be easy to pick up. I'm more interested in what happened here. Let's have some light. I want to take a look at the face of this guy I've brought in.'

A match scraped and Bradley lit a lamp. He held it over the dead man, and whistled through his teeth when he got a look at the upturned face.

'It's Charlie Parker,' said Truscott, and added: 'One of Hank Whiteman's crew.'

'I thought I recognized Buck Whiteman's voice giving orders,' Bradley said.

'We'd better take a look at the others out front,' Morgan suggested.

'I'll take care of it.' Truscott took the lamp and went out to the street, his pistol ready in his right hand.

Morgan covered the deputy from the doorway of the office, explaining to Bradley what they had discovered out at Ashby's ranch.

'So Mulder is still alive,' Bradley mused. 'Heck, that is good news. I'm happy for Jenny's sake.'

'Mulder was mad as hell at having been held prisoner. But he says he doesn't know what happened the night Wishart was killed, and I see no reason to doubt him. When he gets here with the prisoners we'll have a tough session interrogating them. It's a good thing you held off that gang. If we'd lost the likes of Jake Billing, Raynor and his two pards Wymer and Benton, my case would have fallen apart.'

'Before I forget,' Bradley said. 'Just before the shooting started I looked in on Jonas Draper and he said he's ready to talk if you'll do a deal with him. He looked really sorry for himself, so you might get something out of him.'

'I'll see him now,' Morgan decided. 'You'd better come and listen to what's said in case I need a witness.'

He took the cell keys and a lamp through to the cells, most of which were occupied, and Bradley followed to stand to one side of the door to Draper's cell. The little lawyer was huddled on his bunk, his face gaunt and pale, his eyes large, overbright. When he saw Morgan, Draper sprang up, came to the door and gripped the bars.

'They were trying to get in here to kill me,' Draper gasped. 'Have they gone now?'

'Those who weren't killed have pulled out,' Morgan replied. 'What's on your mind, Draper? I'm a mite busy at the moment and I ain't got time to beat about the bush. If you've got something to say then get on with it. It's round-up time. The chickens are coming home to roost.'

'I'll do a deal with you,' Draper said.

'What have you got to trade?' Morgan grimaced. 'If you have information that will help me nail the men responsible for the trouble around here then I'll see that the judge hears of your public-spirited action, and I have no doubt he'll take it into consideration when setting your sentence. You know that's the way it's done, so spill what you know, if you've got anything worthwhile to tell. But be warned — don't waste my time.'

'I was dragged into this against my will.' Draper sighed heavily. 'I'm sure they would have killed me if I hadn't gone along with them. I didn't think Wishart would get shot. He wasn't supposed to have gone down to the bank the night they planned to rob it. Billing had special keys cut for his gang to get in there. But Whiteman could not resist the chance to dig at Mulder, and he overplayed his hand that night, with the result that Wishart and Mulder went down into the thick of the robbery. But things had been getting out of hand. They brought in killers and outlaws, and nobody was safe when Ashby engaged Frayne to keep people in line.'

'Start at the beginning,' Morgan suggested. 'But keep it short for now.'

'Hank Whiteman started it. He wanted the Mulder ranch, and when his ridiculous offers for the spread didn't pay off he decided to force the issue. It was his idea to keep baiting Mulder until he didn't know where he was, but Mulder's got more than his fair share of pride and swallowed the bait hook, line and sinker. I didn't know all the details of their plan, and I was shocked when the shots were fired down in the bank. But I wasn't surprised. The whole thing had become a nightmare. Ashby and Whiteman were handling it jointly and it wasn't working out properly. I was forced to go along with them as far as the legal side of it was concerned, and they used threats to get me to do what they wanted. I knew Dan Meeker was Jake Billing, the outlaw, and he organized everything.'

'Will you make a statement listing these details?' Morgan demanded.

'Gladly. I was a fool to listen to them. Now my life is in danger, and I want to see the end of this.'

Morgan turned to Bradley. 'Did you hear all that, Mike?' he demanded.

'Sure thing,' the deputy replied. 'I

guess it answers a lot of questions, huh?'

'It'll help a great deal,' Morgan replied.

They went back into the office and Truscott turned from the open doorway. 'A rider has just ridden along the street,' he reported. 'It looked like Ashby. He sure took his time coming into town. You want me to pick him up? He's supposed to be under arrest, ain't he?'

Morgan shook his head. 'It's my job,' he said. 'I'll get him. You'd better stay here in case some more of Whiteman's men show up.'

Truscott was disappointed, and Morgan left the office and went along the sidewalk to the saloon. He peered into the long bar through a window in an alley. A large crowd was inside, drinking and discussing the shooting, but there was no sign of Ashby. Morgan went along the alley to the back lots and stood in the shadows until his eyes became accustomed to his surroundings. He heard a horse stamp, and eventually detected the shape of an animal standing beyond the back door of the saloon.

Moving forward silently, Morgan was only feet from the door when a harsh voice spoke to him from the blackness.

'Hold it. I got a gun on you. Who are you and what do you want?'

'I've got a message for Ashby from Draper.' Morgan spoke without hesitation, and kept moving forward.

'Draper is in jail. How'd you get to talk to him?'

'Who do you work for?' Morgan countered. 'Ashby or Whiteman?'

'Whiteman, of course. Who pays your wages?'

'Ashby, so let me in. I saw Ashby riding along the street a few minutes ago, and he'll want to know what I've learned.'

'I'll take you to him. Come on in.'

The shadows were dispelled as the man turned and opened the back door, permitting a shaft of yellow light to stab out of the saloon. Morgan palmed his gun and jabbed the muzzle against the man's spine.

'Keep going,' he said, snatching the man's pistol from his grasp. 'I want Ashby.'

The man walked to Ashby's office and thrust open the door. He entered, and Morgan saw Ashby crouching in front of an open safe, emptying the contents into two saddle-bags. The saloonman turned at the noise of their entrance, and his mouth gaped when he recognized Morgan. He straightened, dropping a wad of greenbacks in his shock.

'Where in hell did you spring from?' he demanded. 'I thought you'd be too busy to bother with me.'

'Caught you red-handed, huh? You didn't think I'd let you get away, did you?' Morgan grinned. 'Draper talked. I know about you and Whiteman planning to steal Mulder's ranch and getting Meeker, alias Jake Billing, to organize the bank job. I got you dead to rights, Ashby. It'll do you no good to protest your innocence now. Get your hands up. Stay quiet and we'll get out of here without half the town knowing about it.'

Ashby turned and picked up his saddlebags despite Morgan's warning to remain still.

'I'll lock these in the safe,' he said. 'There's fifty thousand dollars here.'

'Does that include some of the money stolen from the bank?' Morgan countered.

Sweat was beading Ashby's face as he thrust the bags into the safe. He slammed the door, locked it and turned to face Morgan with the keys held out in his left hand. As Morgan reached for the keys, Ashby brought up his right hand, revealing a Remington .22, which he levelled at Morgan.

Morgan fired instinctively. His bullet ploughed into Ashby's chest, rocking the office with its deadly report. Ashby was slammed back against the safe by the impact, and Morgan hurled himself sideways as the .22 spurted flame and smoke. The bullet hit Morgan in the left side of the chest. Morgan sprawled against the desk and overbalanced. He fell to the floor, teeth clenched against the pain blossoming in his chest, but had the presence of mind to keep the guard in view. He saw the man making a dive for the office doorway.

'Hold it!' Morgan yelled, and fired again when the man ignored him, aiming for the right leg. The bullet caught the man in the back of the thigh almost in the instant of his disappearing into the passage. He lurched against the doorpost, then twisted and fell.

Morgan pressed his left hand against his ribs, feeling the stickiness of oozing blood on his jacket. He sat down on the edge of the desk, thankful that Ashby had not used a .45, and gazed broodingly at the motionless body of the saloonman, lying on its back with arms outflung. There was a big splotch of blood in the centre of Ashby's chest. He was dead or unconscious.

Morgan heard running footsteps in

the passage and levelled his gun at the doorway. A head was thrust around the doorjamb and Morgan recognized Billy Scarfe. Seeing Morgan, Scarfe came into the room, then halted abruptly and gazed intently at Ashby.

'So you finally caught up with him, huh?' he observed. 'Is he dead?'

'I ain't checked him yet,' Morgan replied. 'Where do you fit into this business?'

'Strictly as an outsider.' Scarfe shook his head. 'I didn't know exactly what was going on, but working here, I picked up a few pointers. I would have left long ago but for my daughter. She's against leaving, and I'd sure as hell like to know who the man is she's seeing on the quiet.'

Morgan put his gun on the desk and opened his jacket to examine his chest. He was losing blood, and was relieved to discover that he had collected a flesh wound, mainly because he had been moving to his right when Ashby fired. He jammed his left elbow against the wound and picked up his gun.

'Send someone for the doctor,' he said, and Scarfe departed swiftly.

Morgan had no need to check Ashby. He could see the saloonman was dead. He crossed to the door, where the guard was groaning and clutching his leg, dragged him into the office and heaved him into a chair.

'Where's Hank Whiteman?' he demanded.

'He ain't around here, that's for sure. He's out at the ranch, I reckon. When he heard you were arresting men connected with the bank robbery he sent his son, Buck, with a dozen of us to bust the prisoners out of jail. Well, he sure made a mistake, huh? You're riding the clean-up trail. You had a big reputation before you got here, but nobody figured you could beat this set-up.'

'It's been a real twisted trail,' Morgan observed. 'But now I've got the rights of it.'

He sat in silence, his shoulders hunched, until footsteps in the passage alerted him. Then Scarfe appeared, followed by Doc Caylin. The doctor checked Ashby and shook his head. He turned to Morgan, enquiry showing on his creased features.

'Who's next?' he demanded crisply.

'Take a look at his leg,' Morgan said. 'I think he's worse off than me.'

Caylin examined the leg in question, then bandaged it. 'I'll have him carried to my office for more treatment,' he said at length. 'You're bleeding, Morgan.'

'It's not serious.' Morgan had difficulty removing his jacket and Billy Scarfe came forward to help him.

At that moment Frank Truscott stepped into the doorway, his expression filled with foreboding. He was relieved by the sight of Morgan sitting up and taking notice, and Morgan grinned at him.

'We heard the shooting from the office,' Truscott said. 'Mike figured I'd better check on it.' He looked down at Ashby's motionless body and shook his head. 'You gave him enough chances to throw in his hand,' he observed. 'It's strange how some men would rather be dead than face failure in their crookedness.'

'What did Ashby shoot you with?' Caylin demanded as he examined Morgan's ribs. 'Looks like he used a peashooter. It's a good thing he didn't tote a .45. The bullet hit the second rib and was turned outwards. It creased the inside of your arm on its way through. You'll be sore for a couple of days, but it'll be healed by the time we bury Ashby.' He set about bandaging the chest wound. 'By the way,' he added, 'I was on my way back to town from seeing Mrs Osbome at the Bar O, and just out of town I was passed by Buck Whiteman and a couple of the HW crew. They were riding hell for leather, heading for HW. I figured the town had caught fire, and was surprised, when I arrived, to find everything looking normal. I guess Buck must have been hell-raising around here before he left, huh? You'd think a man like Hank

Whiteman would put a curb on his only son.'

'Nothing will save father and son now,' Morgan said heavily. 'Buck's been attacking the jail on his father's orders. Wanted to release my prisoners. I'll be riding out to arrest them as soon as I can get around to it. By the way, Doc, how is Sheriff Cassidy?'

'He'll be all right. It'll take him a couple of weeks to get back on his feet. But things should be quieter around here by then, huh?'

'You said it.' Morgan got to his feet, moving his left arm experimentally. 'Thanks, Doc. It doesn't feel too bad now. I'm thinking of showing up at HW around dawn for the final showdown.'

'Shall I gather a posse together?' Truscott asked eagerly. 'I reckon we'll need twenty, mebbe thirty men to handle it. Whiteman runs a big crew these days, and nobody will quit. It'll have to be done the hard way.'

'Let's go back to the office and talk about it,' Morgan said. 'Scarfe, it might be a good idea to close the saloon now Ashby's dead.'

'Sure.' Scarfe took a last look at Ashby's body and departed, shaking his head.

Morgan picked up his pistol and checked it, refilling empty chambers.

'Is this man your prisoner?' Caylin asked, jerking a thumb at the wounded gunman. 'I need to do some more work on his leg. You can safely leave him at my place. He ain't gonna be walking anywhere with that wound.'

Morgan nodded. 'Anything you say, Doc,' he responded. 'The jail's about full now. If I take any more prisoners we'll have a real problem accommodating them.'

Truscott accompanied him and they went through to the bar. Scarfe was ushering out the protesting patrons, and grinned when Morgan bellied up to the bar. He poured drinks for the two lawmen, and helped himself to whiskey.

'I always knew Ashby would come to a bad end,' Scarfe said.

'Lock the place and leave the keys in the law office,' Morgan retorted, gulping a much-needed whiskey. He walked to the batwings, followed by Truscott.

The town was quiet in the darkness. Morgan stifled a yawn. There was the reek of gunsmoke in the air. He steeled himself to go on. It had been a long day, but he knew from experience that the showdown was yet to come.

10

Truscott was disappointed when Morgan vetoed his suggestion that they raise a large posse and ride out to HW. Bradley shrugged and waited for Morgan to explain his thoughts.

'We don't want a war out there,' Morgan said, 'and that's what we'd get if we took a posse along. I reckon two of us should be enough to do what I have in mind, and I'll take someone with me because I need a guide to HW. Apart from that, I always work alone, so who's gonna ride with me?'

'Frank will,' Bradley said.

Morgan smiled. 'I could do with a fresh horse,' he told Truscott. 'Can you do something about that?'

'I'll attend to it now.' Truscott shook his head ruefully. 'Just the two of us riding out to HW, huh? That should be mighty interesting.'

'And I'll be going into the ranch alone,' Morgan said pointedly.

'Sure. You want me to stand by and pick up your pieces afterwards, huh?' Truscott grinned and departed.

'I suggest you get at least six men in here for the rest of the night,' Morgan said, and Bradley nodded. 'I've got a feeling that Whiteman won't let the matter rest where it is. The doctor said he saw Buck Whiteman and two men splitting the breeze back to HW. I think they'll pick up more men and come back in force. They've got to kill us to conceal their guilt.'

'I can get some of the men who normally stand by for posse work,' Bradley said. 'I'll send Ike Sayer to round them up.'

'Is he back from Ashby's place?'.

'Yeah, he rode in about five minutes ago. Brought some more prisoners.'

'Where's Gus Mulder and Jenny?'

'They didn't come into town with Sayer. Gus wanted to get back to his place. Perhaps he's gone to fetch his crew. Knowing him, he'd want to be in at the kill.'

'I hope he won't go off half-cocked,' Morgan mused. 'But I wouldn't blame him if he did.'

Bradley went to the door leading to the cells and called to the night jailer, who was in the cell block. There was a short discussion, and Sayer left the office hurriedly. Bradley came back to Morgan, who was sitting on a corner of the desk, favouring his left side.

'You really think we could be in for some more gun trouble?' Bradley asked.

'That's the way I read it.' Morgan nodded. 'The Whitemans are in this up to their necks, and Hank is the only one of the gang on the outside at the moment. When he gets word of what happened here he's gonna come running with every gun he can muster to put us out of business and free the prisoners. If he manages to do that he might just keep the law off his neck. I don't see any other course of action open to him. So you've got a big night to get through, and you better impress that on anyone who turns up to help you.'

'You haven't got statements from any of the prisoners yet,' Bradley observed.

'We know the rights of the business now, and while Hank Whiteman is on the loose I guess everything else can wait. If I get Whiteman tonight there'll be plenty of time tomorrow to worry about statements.'

The sound of a pistol hammering three times sent a string of echoes across the town. Morgan got to his feet, hand dropping instinctively to his holster. He grunted at the pain that stabbed through his left side. The wound was stiffening, and that meant trouble for him.

'That could be Frank in trouble,' Bradley said.

'I'll check it out.' Morgan went to the door and eased out to the sidewalk. He paused and placed his back to the front wall of the building, then looked around, but darkness was cloaking the town and he listened for a moment to the fading gun echoes grumbling away into the distance. Forcing himself to move quickly, he crossed the street and walked along the opposite sidewalk towards the stable. Here and there dark figures were standing on the sidewalk, their excited voices questioning the shots. But no one was making any effort to locate the disturbance.

When he reached the end of the sidewalk, where the prairie commenced, Morgan crossed the street again and walked to the big front doorway of the stable. Two horses were standing to one side of the doorway, their reins trailing, and a motionless figure lay in the pool of light cast by the lantern high up on the doorpost.

Morgan looked around carefully before closing in on the body, and a sigh escaped him when he recognised Frank Truscott. A swift examination revealed that the deputy was dead. Morgan moved out of the lamplight and stood in the shadows, looking around and listening intently. He wondered if Truscott had been killed to lure him out into the open, and here he was at the scene, like a lamb that had been led to slaughter. But nothing happened and he fetched the horses and led them back into the barn. He heard footsteps approaching, and then the doctor appeared, medical bag in hand.

'He didn't stand a chance,' Caylin said after a swift examination. 'Three bullets in the back at close range. He was dead before he hit the ground.'

'I'm wondering who shot him.' Morgan was trying to pierce the gloom beyond the radius of the lamplight, and suddenly saw wisps of straw falling to the ground from the loft. His teeth clicked together when he recalled Mull Johnson. 'Hey, Johnson,' he yelled. 'I know you're up in the loft. Get down here at once. I want to talk to you.' His voice echoed in the surrounding darkness as he awaited a reply, but silence followed his words.

The doctor picked up his bag and moved away.

'There's nothing else I can do here,' he said hurriedly. 'Be careful how you handle Johnson. He's plumb loco. I wouldn't trust him in any situation.'

Morgan nodded, and waited until the sound of the doctor's footsteps had faded away. He drew his gun and cocked it.

'Don't make me come up after you, Johnson,' he warned. 'If you didn't shoot Truscott then you must have seen who did. I thought Truscott was your friend. Why did you kill him?'

'I didn't mean to.' Johnson's voice was filled with anger. 'He came in for those horses, and he said I could hang for killing Frayne. But I told you Dan Meeker killed Frayne. I ain't gonna be railroaded for something I didn't do.'

'So you shot Truscott. You better get down here so I can lock you in the jail for your own protection.'

Johnson uttered a cry of defiance, and Morgan eased backwards into heavy shadow. He had barely moved when a gun cut loose from the loft, blasting out the silence and lashing the darkness with orange muzzleflame. Bullets crackled and screeched around Morgan. He quickly canted the muzzle of his .44 and fired twice at the gun flashes overhead. A choked cry sounded, and then Johnson's big body came pitching out of the loft to thud on the ground only feet from where Morgan was standing.

Morgan turned the big man over and looked into his pallid face. Johnson was dead, and Morgan wondered how, with his childlike mind, the man had got mixed up in the crookedness that flourished in Turkey Creek. He was still gazing down upon the dead man when the doctor returned.

'I can guess what kind of a night this is gonna be,' Caylin said. He did not bother to examine Johnson. 'Did you have to shoot him? Mentally, he was just a big kid. His brain stopped developing when he fell on his head.'

'He was shooting at me,' Morgan said roughly. 'And I've run out of time. I couldn't waste any more of it trying to talk him out of the loft, and I couldn't leave him with a gun.'

He turned and left the barn, walking swiftly despite the pain of his wound, hurrying to get back to the law office, and as he reached the door he heard the sound of approaching hoofs in the distance, rapidly drumming nearer. He thrust open the door to find Mike Bradley pacing the office, a Winchester tucked under his right arm.

'Riders coming,' Morgan said curtly. 'A great number of them.'

'We're ready for anything now,' Bradley retorted. 'Ike managed to get seven men to come with him, and they're all in the cell block, loaded for bear. What was that shooting about?'

Morgan saw the light die out of Bradley's eyes when he explained about Truscott. But there was no time to dwell on the subject.

'I'm gonna stay out here in the town,'

Morgan said. 'If they start shooting up the jail again I'll pinpoint the ringleaders and nail them.'

'That's a good idea.' Bradley nodded. 'Good luck.'

Morgan faded back into the shadows and paused to listen. The riders were coming into the street now. He heard Bradley thrust home the bolts on the inside of the office door, and a moment later the lamp in the office was extinguished. He moved away quickly, his left arm pressed against his ribs to ease the pain.

There were no townsmen on the street now. Morgan walked towards the stable. He could see about twelve riders milling around there, visible in the light of the single lantern. He drew his .44, and checked the weapon as he lengthened his stride. He wanted Hank Whiteman and, although this was not the ideal time to arrest the rancher, he knew that with the HW rancher out of it the outfit would most likely decline to fight.

Truscott's body in the doorway of the stable had stopped the riders for the moment and, as he neared the spot, Morgan could hear a discussion going on. He recognized Hank Whiteman's booming voice ringing through the darkness, and then spotted the big rancher on his horse in the lamplight, waving a pistol to emphasize his words. He suddenly became aware of a man hurrying towards the stable some yards ahead, and when the man began shouting at Hank Whiteman, Morgan recognized the voice as Billy Scarfe's.

'You've got to know the latest, Hank,' Scarfe yelled. 'Ashby is dead, gunned down in his office by the Pinkerton man. Everyone else in the gang is dead or in jail. Mulder has been turned loose from Ashby's ranch, and the first thing he'll do is bring his outfit after you for a reckoning. It's the end of the trail for you. The law has got the deadwood on you. It's fight or run time.'

A silence descended over the riders as the news was assimilated. Morgan stepped aside into an alley mouth and remained watching. Hank Whiteman was tall in his saddle, head and shoulders over most of his crew. He cursed long and hard as he considered.

'Well that does it,' he said at length. 'There ain't nothing for it but to bust open the jail. Waco, take some men and cover the back of the place. Start pouring lead into them. Buck, you take six men along the street and pump some shots into the front office. This time you shoot real hell out of the place. We'll move in when you've softened them up. Duffy, take a couple of men and go to the gunsmith's. Bust in and grab all the cartridges you can lay your hands on and pass them out among the boys. Come on, get to it. I want this business settled before dawn. By then we'll either be in the clear or dead.'

Men detached themselves from the group and rode off to do the rancher's bidding. Four men remained, among them Billy Scarfe. Hank Whiteman dismounted and stood over Truscott's body. Moments later, shooting sounded from along the street and echoes rolled across the town.

Morgan thought over his priorities and decided to arrest the three men sent to break into the gunsmith's shop. If the HW crew were low on cartridges it would be sensible to restrict their supply. He sneaked out of the alley and ran along the sidewalk until he saw the gunsmith's sign. The shooting along the street was growing in intensity as he drew his pistol and walked in through the open doorway of the shop.

Someone had lit a lamp on the counter, and the men were busy thrusting boxes of cartridges into gunny sacks. Morgan cocked his gun, the sound lost in the shooting. But one of the men spotted him and swung, reaching for his holstered gun. Morgan fired instantly and the man dropped. The other two let go of their sacks and raised their hands. Morgan closed in and struck with the muzzle of his pistol,

248

catching the nearest man a swinging blow against the right temple that sent him sprawling against his companion as he collapsed. Morgan hit the second man before he could disentangle himself from his pard, and then checked the man he had shot, finding him to be dead.

Moving quickly, Morgan bent over the unconscious men and removed their guns. He looked around the shop, found a rope, and bound the men's hands behind their backs. He left the shop, closed the door, then went back along the sidewalk towards the stable. The shooting around the jail had become fast and furious, and Morgan lengthened his stride.

He reached the end of the sidewalk and stopped in surprise, for Hank Whiteman and his men were now standing in line in the doorway of the barn, facing three riders who had ridden in from out of town. The newcomers were holding drawn pistols. Narrowing his eyes, Morgan recognized the foremost rider as Gus Mulder, who was talking, and he listened for a moment.

'It's about time you were stopped in your tracks, Whiteman,' the Big G rancher was saying. 'I got the rights of it now. You're the kingpin behind all this trouble, and it was all because of my spread. But it went wrong for you when the Pinkerton detective showed up. He got Ashby dead to rights, and if I know Ashby he won't stall for long. He'll spill his guts to save his own neck. But I don't need a detective to fight my battles for me. I'm calling you out. You've come to the end of your rope, mister.'

Mulder swung out of his saddle, holstered his gun, and stepped forward from his horse, ready to fight.

'Go to it,' he rapped. 'I'm giving you more chance than you gave poor Lew Wishart.'

'Do you think I'm afraid of you?' Whiteman demanded, crouching a little. His right hand moved a fraction towards the flared butt of the sixgun holstered on his hip. 'I've been praying for the day when I could see you through gunsmoke.'

'So quit stalling,' Mulder rapped. 'Turn her loose.'

Morgan wanted Whiteman alive, and cocked his gun as he stepped from the shadows.

'Hold it right there,' he called, and all eyes turned to him. 'Personally, I feel you have a moral right to kill Whiteman, but as a lawman I got to tell you that I need him alive. So let's forget about gunplay, huh?'

'You did me a big favour earlier, Morgan,' Mulder responded, 'and I'll be grateful for the rest of my life. But you ain't gonna cheat me of this pleasure. Whiteman is a snake, and I'm gonna finish him.'

'You'll have to fight me afterwards,' Morgan rapped, 'and I got you pegged as a law-abiding man. Listen to the shooting that's going on. It's Whiteman's crew trying to bust into the jail to kill the prisoners and destroy the evidence I've got. Take Whiteman prisoner and you'll have the pleasure of watching him hang in due course.'

'No one's gonna put a rope around my neck,' Whiteman snarled, and reached for his gun. His draw was surprisingly fast for a big man. His pistol cleared leather and swung up to cover Mulder, who had been galvanized into action by Whiteman's movement.

But it was one of the Whiteman's men who proved to be even faster. His gun seemed to leap into his hand and he blasted off a shot even as Morgan reacted and fired. The gunman's slug struck Mulder in the instant that Morgan's bullet took him in the chest, and both men went down together. Whiteman turned instantly and fled. Morgan, intent on the shooting, caught the HW rancher's movement out of the corner of his eye and, by the time he turned to bring the man under his muzzle, Whiteman had dived sideways beyond the corner of the doorway and disappeared into the barn. Morgan's instinct was to pursue Whiteman, but he could not turn his back on Whiteman's two men standing in the doorway. He called to Mulder's pair of riders.

'One of you check Mulder,' he rapped. 'The other can hold these prisoners until I've got time to deal with them.'

Both riders dismounted quickly. Morgan was covering the two HW men and Billy Scarfe, who was standing motionless beside them.

'Get rid of your guns,' Morgan ordered, and the men divested themselves of weapons. Scarfe opened his jacket and produced a pistol from a shoulder holster, which he threw down on the ground. 'Scarfe, you'd better get out of here,' Morgan decided. 'I'll talk to you later.'

'I'm not mixed up in this,' Scarfe said, and took to his heels, vanishing quickly into the shadows.

Morgan fought his impatience and

crossed to where the cowpuncher was checking the prostrate Mulder. The man looked up, his face pale in the dim lamplight.

'I think the boss will make it,' he said. 'But I better fetch the doctor pronto.'

'What are you waiting for?' Morgan demanded.

The man got up and ran off along the street. Morgan turned and went into the stable. He wanted Hank Whiteman.

The stable was dark. Morgan paused until his eyes became accustomed to the gloom then went to the back door. He dashed outside and flattened himself against the back wall, gun raised, eyes narrowed. The shooting around the jail had settled into a steady exchange of fire between Whiteman's crew and the lawmen inside, the sound of shots hammering and echoing. Morgan was certain Whiteman was doomed to failure, for the rancher could not know the strength Bradley had at his command. But Whiteman was past caring about odds. He was desperate.

A faint breeze was blowing into Morgan's face, laced with drifting gunsmoke. He walked steadily along the back lots, keeping close to the rear of the buildings fronting the street. Reaching the back of the saloon, he paused and tried the door. It was locked. He checked his surroundings, then went on.

He heard the sound of voices for an instant as he neared the back of the hotel, and froze, his breathing restrained while he listened intently. There was a lull in the shooting around the jail, and as the echoes faded away the silence became intense. But he saw and heard nothing, and wondered who was waiting for him in the shadows. He dropped to one knee and used his eyes, searching the area thoroughly, his life depending on his vigilance.

He heard a faint sound as of a body moving impatiently somewhere ahead, perhaps in the back doorway of the hotel. Had Whiteman chosen this spot to turn at bay? He clenched his fingers tightly around the butt of his .44 and arose to go on. He was now barely five yards from the door of the hotel. But before he could move a voice hissed in an undertone from the darkness ahead.

'Who's out there?' The voice was hoarse with fear. 'I can hear you. Is it Morgan?'

Morgan dropped to one knee, gun ready, his finger trembling on the trigger.

'This is Amos Henty.' The voice was pitched a little higher, filled with desperation. 'I need to talk to you, Morgan. You might think I'm mixed up in this bad business but I'm not involved. Draper dragged me into it.'

Morgan shook his head impatiently. Henty was small fry, and could be picked up at any time. But Morgan was too careful to take chances. He dropped flat to the ground and pushed his pistol out in front of his body, covering the vital area before him.

'It's Morgan,' he called. 'Henty, come on out with your hands raised.'

At his words the night was split by gun flame and bullets sped through the darkness at about waist high. A gun was emptied at Morgan from the black pile of the hotel sending a string of shots hammering through the night above Morgan, who angled his gun slightly and returned fire, aiming for the centre of the orange flashes that were tearing a hole in the shadows. The shooting cut out abruptly, and echoes fled across the town. Morgan reloaded his pistol and pushed himself to one knee. There was deathly silence now, and Morgan's ears were ringing from the shock of the rapid detonations.

He crawled forward slowly, his gun ready, and froze when his left hand touched a face that was upturned to the sky. His gun swung in towards the man's head but he witheld the blow for there was no movement, and he realized that death had occurred.

'Are you still alive, Morgan?' Henty demanded, and Morgan swung his gun up to cover the speaker. 'Billy Scarfe came into the hotel a few minutes ago, with Hank Whiteman following him. Whiteman told us pull you into a trap. But you've hit Scarfe. He's down, and I hope he's dead.'

'Where's Whiteman?' Morgan demanded.

'He's gone to the jail. You'll have to kill him to stop him now. He's over the edge, past reasoning.'

'Then get back into the hotel and stay there until I come for you,' Morgan rapped. 'I got my hands full right now, but I'll get around to you.'

The sound of a door opening and then closing came to Morgan's ears and he reloaded his pistol before easing forward and going on. He saw gun flashes ahead and closed in silently until he was standing within feet of the nearest man firing at the back of the jail. He counted five different guns attacking the building, and fired without warning, aiming for gun flashes, and two of the guns ceased firing almost immediately. He continued to shoot at gun flashes until the attack stopped.

One of the attackers called out, demanding to know what was going on, and Morgan reloaded his .44 before fading into the alley beside the jail and making his way towards the street. There were at least six guns firing steadily into the front of the law office with three weapons returning fire.

Before Morgan could get into the fight he saw a figure coming towards his position in the mouth of the alley. He eased back a pace, lifting his gun. He had not been seen, and he held his fire, recognizing the big figure of Hank Whiteman himself. The shooting eased at that moment and someone in the shadows on the opposite side of the street called out.

'Where you going, Pa?'

Whiteman paused only feet from Morgan and turned to face his son, who came running towards him. 'There's no shooting at the back of the jail,' he replied. 'I wanta know what's going on. When I come back we're gonna burn down the jail. That'll bring 'em out. We'll burn the whole town if we have to.'

Morgan waited for Whiteman to face him again, and when the rancher came on to the alley he showed himself, gun ready.

'You're finished, Whiteman,' Morgan said. 'Throw down your gun and tell your men to stop shooting.'

Whiteman froze in shock, then uttered a curse and swung up his gun. Morgan was waiting, aware that the rancher would not submit to arrest, and just before Whiteman's gun was levelled he fired, aiming for the centre of the man's chest. Whiteman took the slug, which knocked him back a couple of steps before his legs gave way and he pitched to the ground.

Buck Whiteman was only a few yards from his father, and stopped to lift his gun, so Morgan fired. The youngster dropped to one knee, hit in the chest, and triggered his gun once before he died. The shooting stopped then, and an uneasy silence settled over Turkey Creek.

'It's all over,' Morgan shouted, his voice echoing across the street. 'Hank Whiteman is dead and Buck is down. You gunnies are out of a job. Come out with your hands up or get to hell out of town.'

He paused, and moments later heard sounds of departing riders as the survivors of the HW crew pulled out. He went out to where Whiteman was lying, and was looking down at the body of the rancher when Mike Bradley pulled open the door of the law office and came out to the sidewalk, followed by the men who had fought with him.

Morgan drew a deep breath into his lungs, suddenly aware that his wound was hurting, and he was tired. But it looked like the end of the trail here. He had the rights of the case and would soon tie up any loose ends. He smiled as Bradley came to him, carrying a rifle.

'Do me a favour, Mike,' he said as the deputy joined him.

'Just name it,' Bradley responded. 'We'd get the moon for you if that was what you wanted.'

'Nothing like that.' Morgan thrust his deadly gun into his holster. 'Don't wire my office and tell them this case is over, huh? Not for a week at least. I reckon they already got something else lined up for me, but I've earned a spell from my job.'

'You got a deal,' Bradley said. 'Anyway, I reckon you'll need a week to get all those statements from the prisoners.'

Morgan nodded. 'That's something I definitely ain't looking forward to,' he said. 'But it looks like the shooting is over so I'm gonna try the bed in my hotel room. This town will be back to normal come morning.'

He squared his shoulders, gritted his teeth against the pain darting through his chest, and strode off along the street, aware that, despite his words to the contrary, the first thing he would do in the morning was send a wire to his head office.

We do hope that you have enjoyed reading this large print book.

Did you know that all of our titles are available for purchase?

We publish a wide range of high quality large print books including:
Romances, Mysteries, Classics
General Fiction
Non Fiction and Westerns

Special interest titles available in large print are:
The Little Oxford Dictionary
Music Book, Song Book
Hymn Book, Service Book

Also available from us courtesy of Oxford University Press:
Young Readers' Dictionary
(large print edition)
Young Readers' Thesaurus
(large print edition)

For further information or a free brochure, please contact us at:
Ulverscroft Large Print Books Ltd.,
The Green, Bradgate Road, Anstey,
Leicester, LE7 7FU, England.
Tel: (00 44) **0116 236 4325**
Fax: (00 44) **0116 234 0205**

A TOWN CALLED
TROUBLESOME

John Dyson

Matt Matthews had carved his ranch out of the wild Wyoming frontier. But he had his troubles. The big blow of '86 was catastrophic, with dead beeves littering the plains, and the oncoming winter presaged worse. On top of this, a gang of desperadoes had moved into the Snake River valley, killing, raping and rustling. All Matt can do is to take on the killers single-handed. But will he escape the hail of lead?

THE WIND WAGON

Troy Howard

Sheriff Al Corning was as tough as they came and with his four seasoned deputies he kept the peace in Laramie — at least until the squatters came. To fend off starvation, the settlers took some cattle off the cowmen, including Jonas Lefler. A hard, unforgiving man, Lefler retaliated with lynchings. Things got worse when one of the squatters revealed he was a former Texas lawman — and no mean shooter. Could Sheriff Corning prevent further bloodshed?

CABEL

Paul K. McAfee

Josh Cabel returned home from the Civil War to find his family all murdered by rioting members of Quantrill's band. The hunt for the killers led Josh to Colorado City where, after months of searching, he finally settled down to work on a ranch nearby. He saved the life of an Indian, who led him to a cache of weapons waiting for Sitting Bull's attack on the Whites. His involvement threw Cabel into grave danger. When the final confrontation came, who had the fastest — and deadlier — draw?